STUBBY'S WAR

A Dog's View of the Great War

Based on a True Story

Diane R. Weber

About this Edition

The dog Stubby was real, and his human, Corporal James Robert Conroy, was a real soldier. The war and the battles Stubby fought in were real. The other characters and events portrayed in this book are fictitious. However, some of the events were inspired by letters and journals of actual soldiers in the war. These soldiers are credited in a section at the end of the book. My addition of Stubby into these events is entirely fictional and is not meant to lessen the bravery of these American heroes in any way. Any historical errors are my own.

No part of this book may be reproduced, or stored in a retrieval system, or transmitted in any form or by any means, electronic, mechanical, photocopying, recording, or otherwise, without express written permission of the publisher.

Copyright © 2023 Diane R Weber
All rights reserved.
Publisher by Pint Bottle Press

ISBN-13: 978-1-945005-07-7

Cover design by: Matt Weber
Printed in the United States of America

DEDICATION

This book is dedicated to my paternal grandfather, Robert Stanley Rawding, who fought with the 26th Division of American Expeditionary Forces and all the other brave soldiers who fought there and to the many who sacrificed their lives so that we may live free.

CONTENTS

PART ONE—I Am a Soldier	Page
1	1
2	5
3	9
4	13
5	19
6	21
7	29
PART TWO – The Trenches	
8	35
9	41
10	47
11	57
12	65
13	73
14	81
15	87
16	91

17	95
18	101

PART THREE – Wounded Warriors

19	103

PART FOUR – Devil Dogs

20	119
21	127
22	135
23	141
24	151
25	155
26	159
27	163

PART FIVE – Partners and Heroes

28	167
29	175

PART SIX—The Real Stubby	181
PART SEVEN – The War in Pictures	199
Resources for Further Study	213

Part One – I Am a Soldier

1

The flickering yellow light casts creeping shadows down my alley. I squeeze myself tighter into the corner of my box, toenails scraping the cardboard. My ears twitch left and right, picking up the soft hoot of a distant owl. A rat skitters across the ground. A low whine drifts through the night. As I huddle against the nip of the Autumn wind, I realize the source of the whimpering. It is me.

I bury my nose under my paw and try to go back to sleep, but images of my Mama drift over me like a choking fog.

My Mama's yelp. . . her fitful biting at the tangled net . . . the cage . . . the hulking man reeking of whiskey and sweat . . .

Dawn breaks. I creep out of my box and give myself a good shake from nose to tail, shuffling off the nightmare. *Be brave,* she'd said. And I try.

By day I dig through garbage cans reeking of rotting vegetables and soured milk, searching for scraps of bread or an old sandwich. At night I sleep in empty crates or crouch in alleyways. When the cold wind whips around, I crawl deeper into a corner, shiver, and wait for the morning sun.

I am alone.

The sun warms my back one morning as I make my daily rounds. A young boy and his mother sit on a park bench, their backs toward me. The mother hands the boy a sandwich. My nostrils twitch. I slurp back the drool. Trying not to rustle the leaves, I creep closer.

I approach the boy's end of the bench, quietly stick my nose over the edge, and give him my best sad eyes. The boy reaches his hand toward my face. I sniff his fingers. *Mmmm. Peanut butter.* The boy glances toward his mother, but she is engrossed in her newspaper. Slowly, the boy tears his sandwich in half and holds out a piece. My body wags back and forth. I take it gently from his hand and pull it into my mouth. The sweetbread mingles with the gooey peanut butter as I chew.

It sticks to the roof of my mouth. I stretch my mouth wide and cluck and curl my tongue. I shake my head fiercely. It's stuck. I roll on my back and paw the air as my tongue digs into the sticky goo. My lips peel back as my jaw stretches side to side. No use. It's stuck. The boy erupts in giggles. His mother looks up from her paper.

"Get away from that stray!" She snaps as she stuffs her own half-eaten sandwich into her bag. She grabs the boy's arm. He flashes a grin and waves as she drags him off. The rest of the boy's sandwich lies on the bench. The peanut butter and sweetbread bring back the drool that unlocks my tongue from the roof of my mouth. In an instant, I snap up the sandwich.

Still hungry, I searched for garbage cans. The scent of ham and cheese wafts out of one. I jump on the side, topple the can, and dig through the rubbish.

Grrrr. A throaty growl freezes me in place. With a low growl of my own, I turn toward the intruder. My ears arch forward, and my tail stands erect.

In front of me looms a huge, snarling gray dog, its paws planted firmly on the ground. His lips curl back, baring long teeth. He lowers his head, death in his glinty eyes.

My ears flatten. My tail drops. With a whine, I step back.

The menace takes a step forward. I take a step back.

He takes another step forward. I spin and retreat down the alley, paws pounding.

When the only footfall I hear is my own, I stop and look back. What I took for a huge gray terror is really no larger than me. With a sidelong stare toward me, he smugly munches the ham and cheese.

Be brave, Mama had said. I skulk back to my box.

STUBBY'S WAR

2

A shrill screech jabs the morning air. In a flash, I shoot out of the alley and follow the sound. In a broad field, packs of young men mill around. The blare shrieks again, and the men line up. I run up and down the side of the field. Never have I seen so many men like these.

Wearing green trousers and khaki jackets, the soldiers fall into lines. Their legs are wrapped with canvas strips from their boots to their knees.

A leader calls out, "Rifle!" They touch the long stick slung over one shoulder.

"Bayonet!" They touch the sharp end of the stick.

"Pistol!" They touch their belt.

The soldiers march as a leader calls out. *One, two, one-two. Left, right. Halt! About face. Forward, march*! Like centipedes, their legs all work in the same direction. *One, two, one-two. Left, right.*

The cadence is hypnotic, and I fall alongside, marking time with my stub of a tail. *One, two. One, two.* My short legs take two steps for every one of the men's, but I keep up. At last, they slow their pace. *Forward, halt! At ease!*

A few fellows drift to the trees lining the field and plop down. Panting, I sit in the shade of a tree and watch. One soldier pulls out a canteen and sucks down a swig of water. I lick my lips. He takes off his cap and wipes his hand across his forehead. He spots me, and his eyes crinkle in a grin.

"Well, look here." The fellow jabs his friend with his elbow. "Here's that dog that was following us."

"Yeah," says his friend. "Keeping up with us, too. A little four-legged soldier."

My ears prick forward.

The first soldier turns back to me. "You hungry, boy? How about some oatcake?"

I sniff. He'd had bacon for breakfast. Brown paper rustles as he takes something from his pocket and unwraps it. It smells sweet. His hand lowers to the ground, cupping the cake. His eyes show no danger, but I stay alert. Keeping my eye on his face, I creep toward his hand.

He holds the cake a little closer. I take a chance. With a quick flick of my tongue, I gulp the cake and scoot back. *Not bacon, but still good.* The soldier laughs.

"Come on, fellow. I'll bet you're thirsty, too." He takes another swig from his canteen. He holds his hand down again, and I step forward. He pours water into his cupped hand, and I lap it right from his palm. The soothing liquid rolls down my throat. I stiffen as his fingers scratch under my chin. His hand moves up and behind my ear.

"Good boy." He scratches my other ear, and I relax. My tail knocks back and forth as I meet the soldier's gaze.

The soldier has a smooth, tan face, with eyes bright and sharp like a bird's.

"You're a stubby little fellow," he says. "Is that your

name, boy? Are you Stubby?"

I wag my stubby tail and lick his salty palm. He tastes kind. I bark approval. *Stubby? I can be Stubby.* I let him do some more scratching.

"Hey, Charlie. Meet my buddy," my soldier calls to a friend wandering over.

"Yeah, I saw him trailing us out there," Charlie says. "Seems to like you, Conroy." Charlie has straw-colored hair and freckles and a quick, one-sided grin. His moves are swift and jumpy – like a puppy. He smells like hot sweat – and chocolate. He fishes a chocolate bar out of his pocket. I sniff. Drool leaks out and rolls down my cheek. *Mmm. Chocolate. I remember my last taste of the stuff. Good now, but bad news later.*

The soldier Conroy stands – tall, muscular, and confident – and hoists his rifle over his shoulder. He runs his hand through his dark hair and adjusts his cap. As he looks down at me, the edges of his lips slip up.

"See you tomorrow, Stubby old boy." My stub wags an answer. I watch as the man Conroy walks away. He's okay, I decide. These boys are okay.

The two-legged soldiers tromp off the field, and I tromp back to my alley. I dig among the trashcans and enjoy the scraps of a peach pie. In the moonlit evening, I curl up in my box.

My nightmares are pushed aside as I march in my sleep. *One, two, one, two....*

STUBBY'S WAR

3

The next day the soldiers return to the field. And the next day, and the next. Every day they drill, and every day I plod alongside. Each time the soldiers take a break, Private Conroy has an oatcake for me. I wolf it down and then look up at him. *Where's the bacon? I know you had bacon this morning.*

For weeks I stick by Conroy, and we become pals. When we rest in the shade, he scratches me just like I like it – behind my ears. As he feeds me an oatcake, he talks to me about his family, about his girl back home. I meet his eyes to let him know I'm listening, and he tells me about the war across the sea where he and his buddies are headed. And sometimes, he brings me bacon. When he does, I reward him with licks across the face.

I'm glad of the relentless training, the constant marching and following orders. It leaves me little time to think about the gnawing emptiness of missing my Mama.

We are partners, Conroy tells me as he rubs my neck. And inside, I feel warm and not alone.

Some of the fellows brag about becoming war heroes. How brave they are going to be. But not Conroy. He just watches the others with wise eyes. I remember my Mama. I want to be brave, too, like Conroy.

The bugle calls and marching drills become easy. I can march, *one-two*. I can *About Face!* I can *Halt!*

One day, Private Conroy decides to teach me a new trick. I know because I can smell bacon in his pocket.

"Salute!" he calls. He clicks his heels and snaps his right hand sharply over his eyebrow. I cock my head and watch. He does it again, and again I cock my head. He looks down at me.

"Okay," he says, "Sit!"

Why didn't he say so? I sit and look up, expecting bacon.

"Good boy."

I like it when he says, "good boy." But I still like bacon better.

"Now, sit up!" Conroy snaps his fingers above my head. I blink, my tongue licking the air. Then he gets it. He reaches into his pocket and comes out with a bite of bacon. He twirls it over my head, and I immediately rear up to reach it.

"Good boy." He drops the delicious morsel into my mouth. I lick my lips and look up for more.

"Sit," he says. And I do it. Easy.

"Sit up." Easy. *Where's the bacon?*

"Now, salute!" Conroy snaps his hand above his brow again. I just cock my head.

He reaches down and puts my right paw above my eye. It stays there for about a second and then slides down.

"Good boy!" He drops a bacon bite into my mouth and puts my paw back over my eye. I'm not sure why he wants to do this, but I let him put my paw there again and again because each time, he gives me bacon! I love this game! Soon I move my own paw.

"Salute!"

I stand up straight, sit back on my hind legs, and rear back, front legs in the air. Then I lift my right paw slightly higher to just over my eyebrow. It's easy to do, but Conroy and his buddies are impressed. So, I do it often, especially when I want some bacon! And the neck-scratching. I like that, too.

One day, instead of trekking back to my alley, I follow Conroy to his tent barracks. It smells like sweaty people feet. Seven soldier boys and a leader sleep in each tent. That's sixteen feet! This means sixteen boots get pulled off... which means the sixteen pairs of sweaty socks fill up the tent. "Pee-you!" they say. But I like the smells. And if these guys are my new pack, I want in, too. I peek in the tent.

Swoosh!

Strong arms snatch me from behind.

STUBBY'S WAR

4

I grapple to get loose, then catch a whiff. *Conroy!*

"Where are you going, partner?" He sets me down and ruffs my ears.

"What's this?" The Sergeant bellows from behind us. I drop my body and gaze upward.

"That's Stubby, Sergeant." Conroy snaps to attention. He salutes, just like he taught me.

"Against regulations," growls the Sergeant.

"Yes, Sergeant."

I trot over to Conroy and stand at attention, too.

The Sergeant glowers at me. I scan his face for a flicker of warmth. I glance at Conroy, still in salute.

Standing up as straight and tall as my legs will let me, I rear back on my haunches. Then, I lift my right paw and rest it a little higher than my eyebrow, keeping my gaze steady at the Sergeant.

The Sergeant glares. My paw starts to slip. He studies me, silent. His eyes crinkle, but his chin stays stiff.

"I've heard about this dog." He pauses. "The boys

like him around." Eyes still on me, he is quiet for a long minute. "Just keep him out of the way."

"Yes, Sergeant." Conroy exhales as the Sergeant turns away.

Starting at my ears, down my back, all the way to my tail, I give my body a good shake. *Whew!*

Conroy stoops and scratches my back. I lick his hand and follow him to his cot. I circle once, circle again, and one more time before curling up and drinking in the scent of his boots.

Life in the training camp is harsh, but my new pack is tough. I lie quietly under Conroy's bunk at night, but my nose and ears take it all in. The boys trade stories of girlfriends and life back home. They talk of being lumberjacks or fishermen or farmers. They all were used to honest, hard work, and rugged country life.

"My kid brother wanted to sign up," says the boy they call Sam. "But I told him nine years old was a little too young." He snorts. "I think he just wanted to get out of feeding the chickens."

Tall and brown, Sam has hard muscles and soft eyes. He speaks with a slow drawl and jokes about missing his grits. He smells strong, mixed with the sweetness of the apple drops he keeps in his pocket.

But Conroy is still the best. I curl up and rest my chin on Conroy's boot, but not to ask for anything. I just like it there.

During the day, long hikes and forced marches become routine. The boys grunt when they drop their heavy backpacks for a break. I'm glad I'm a dog and can trot around freely without having to lug one.

We trek back to camp, and I hear my favorite call — the mess call. The boys share their chow with me. They know I don't like the beans, but sometimes they laugh and try to get me to eat them. Of course, I let them smell them again later in the tent. "Pee-you!" they say.

When he can, the cook saves me a bone. Those days are heaven, and I gnaw it all evening. Sometimes I stuff it under Conroy's bunk to save for later.

After my pack goes to sleep, I patrol the barracks. It's my job to keep my boys safe. If I catch the scent of something unusual, aside from the men snoring or breaking wind, I give a low growl. If that doesn't wake Conroy, I let out some deep barks. That gets everyone swearing and stumbling around in a hurry.

Woof! I call out one evening. A deer is crossing our camp. I want Conroy to see it.

Woof!

Conroy scrambles out of the tent, hoisting his rifle, followed by Sam and Charlie. Some others drag out of the tent, half asleep.

Woof!

I point my nose toward the deer. Its white tail catches the moonlight.

Woof! I wag my tail.

The boys just spit and glare at me.

"Stinking deer!" Charlie hisses like an angry cat. "Dang dog! Waking us in the middle of the night."

Conroy scowls. "No, Stubby," he snaps. "No barking. You get back in there and lie down."

I slink down with a jab of that alone feeling in my belly. My thoughts slip back to my Mama: *Me racing down the road, kicking up dirt beneath my paws and sucking in the wind. The truck ... and Mama ... growing tiny in the distance ....*

A little whine slips out as I go back under Conroy's bunk. He flops down with a sigh, but soon his hand reaches under the cot and scratches my chin. I lick his palm.

Some days later, Conroy and Charlie practice on the rifle range, and I follow. They hoist their rifles and fire.

Bang!

Yelp! I jump back. Those things bark loud! From my nose to my tail, every muscle in me wants to turn tail and run. Conroy spots me cowering next to a tree.

"Easy, boy." He rubs my back and neck. "You've got to get used to this if you're going to be a soldier dog."

The shots ring sharp, and I don't like them. But Conroy's voice calms me, and I gradually grow used to the sound of gunfire. Charlie earns what he calls his Expert Medal with the rifle, but I trust Conroy to have my back. And I have his.

After a couple of months, my boys are in shape and are sworn into federal service. Conroy says we are the 102nd United States Infantry and part of The United States Army, 26th Division.

But most people just call us the "Yankee Division."

"Word is, we've got a new commander," Conroy announces one day as he spoons in his beef stew one evening. He ignores my drooling. We've been hiking all day, and I've smelled that beef for the last mile. Next to bacon, beef is my favorite. I lap the air as the sweet scent swirls toward me.

"Here, boy." Sam tears off a hunk of bread, sops it in his stew, and holds it down. I turn my tail to Conroy and trot over to Sam.

Oh, yeah! Beef! I lick Sam's fingers to let him know how much I like him tonight. I cut a glance toward Conroy. *Where's your beef?* my eyes ask. But he doesn't notice me.

"Major General Edwards," says Charlie. "I hear his last company liked him fine — some even called him 'Daddy.'"

"We don't need a Daddy." Sam jabs the air with his crust. "Just someone who knows what he's doing over there." I stroke his leg with my paw to let him know I'm ready for another bite of beef.

"We'll find out soon enough." Conroy's voice trails off. "We'll find out." Finally, he remembers me! "Here, boy." He sets his plate on the ground.

I wolf down the beef bits and the bread before he can change his mind. Then I lick the plate clean as a week-old bone, savoring every bite of the beefy gravy.

One evening before sundown, we break camp at Yale Field and march down to what the boys call Winchester Arms railroad. I hear whispers about secret orders to entrain, but I don't know what that means.

I line up with Conroy, expecting us to start marching. He tosses his duffel into the train car, then turns and kneels next to me.

"Sorry, old boy," he says. "I've got to go. They say no dogs are allowed on the ship." Conroy grabs my cheeks in his fists and gazes at me with sad eyes. "But you'll be all right. You'll stay in the camp, and they will take care of you."

Sensing his heart beating faster as he scratches behind my ears, I meet his eyes. Conroy drops his gaze. With one quick motion, he whips around and jumps into the black hole of the train car.

STUBBY'S WAR

5

My gut knots. *Conroy can't leave me. I'm a soldier, too! I'm his partner!*

I snake through the forest of legs in front of the train car. I spot my chance, dive through the black hole, and land in a panting heap on the floor. But before I can scoot into the corner and hide, Conroy spots me. He slips over. With a stealthy glance around, Conroy reaches down. He swoops his arms around my belly in one smooth move and stuffs me under his coat.

"All right, buddy," he whispers. "We'll give it a try." Under his coat, I feel Conroy's tenseness. I smell his nervous sweat. I lie still and force myself to keep quiet.

The train whistle shrieks, and we chug down the track. I snuggle around until I'm comfortable under Conroy's coat and don't make a sound. As the train rocks back and forth through the countryside, I hear the boys tell stories and brag about how they all are going to be heroes – how they will "Whip the *Boche*!" Then they break into singing:

Over there, over there
Send the word, send the word over there
That the Yanks are coming...

The boys bellow the last line:

And we won't come back till it's over - over there!

My heart beats faster. I think about my Mama. *I'll be brave, Mama. I'll be a hero – like Conroy.*

Conroy keeps me tucked out of sight until we get to the shipyard in Virginia, and I'm glad to finally stop. All that jerking and swaying makes me queasy. I could use a long drink and a few bites of grass. We jump off, and Conroy lets me down. Scampering quickly to the bushes, I sniff around and find my spot. Another dog's been here. I raise my leg and pee. Now he knows *I've* been here. As I trot back, I see Conroy whispering to a ship's crewman, who nods and glances my way. Conroy stuffs me back under his coat. We follow the crewman and slip on board a vessel that Conroy calls the *USS Minnesota*.

When the others go down to stuff their gear in the bunk room of the ship, Conroy holds me tight under his coat and follows the crewman along the deck. We stop, and I hear the scrape of metal. Gently Conroy lowers me down into a pitch-black coal bin. I wiggle my legs and paw at Conroy's arms, but he shushes me. I suck in coal dust and sneeze.

"Don't make a sound." His voice is stern. "No sound." I sit still and look up at him, tilting my head in question. "Be brave, little fella – and be quiet."

Conroy nods to the crewman, then metal *scrraapes* across metal . . . and blocks out the light.

6

I am alone again. The bin is cold and dark. The ship lurches forward, and I trip on sharp coals. I give a tiny *yelp*! The only answer is the chug, chugging of the engine as we leave the port. I struggle to find a spot comfortable to sit.

Why did Conroy leave me?

In the dusty blackness, shards of coal cut into my paws as the ship tosses on the waves. I take a step and stumble. Another jab to my rear leg. I kick out, and the coal rocks clang against the metal sides. At last, the ship settles to a rhythmic rocking, and I find my balance and huddle on the coal. With each breath, my nose sucks up soot. I stifle a sneeze.

Silent, Conroy said. I must be silent.

I wait. I circle and circle in place, finally pushing aside the sharpest coals and nestling down, uncomfortable. I paw at my ear. The ship pitches again. I clamp my jaw and don't make a sound. I bite at my paw to comfort myself.

Trying to remain still, I close my eyes and try to remember Spring. Chasing lizards. Dropping my wiggling prize in front of Mama, watching it scamper off as she licks my face with kisses. I finally drift to sleep.

The ship yaws, and I'm wrenched awake with gnawing images of Mama. *The heavy net as it swoops down over her. The stench of whiskey and sweat as the giant man looms over her. Her painful yelps as he grabs her and throws her into a wire cage. Her sad eyes. Then Conroy's eyes, anxious and stern, as he shuts out the light.*

Be brave.

Alone, I sit swallowed in darkness. Faint cracks of light around the bin door hold out hope, but the light dims as I wait. The ship pitches, and a tiny *yip!* escapes before I can catch it. I sit and clamp my jaws tight. All is silent except for the faint *whup, whup* of the waves against the hull.

I wait. I catch a whiff of a rat. My stomach flutters. Empty. But I mustn't hunt.

I really, really need to pee. Carefully, I pick my way to the other side of the bin and relieve myself. The scent of pee is pungent and follows me as I find my way back to my spot.

Be brave, Conroy said. *But where is he?*

I feel more alone than ever before. My paw itches, and I bite it with my front teeth. I bite, and I bite, a little sharper each time until the pain distracts me and comforts me. I squeeze myself small in the darkness.

At last, I hear steps. My ears twitch, searching for sounds. I sniff. Through the sooty air, I detect a welcome scent. My ears pivot. *Voices.*

Sccrraape.

Metal again scrapes across metal . . . *Conroy!*

Conroy pulls open the bin door.

I leap into his arms, streaking black soot across his shirt. Outside is almost as dark now as inside the coal bin. But I don't care. I am out! I lick my boy's face.

"Shhh, boy," Conroy whispers. He stuffs me under his coat and takes me to his bunk. I drink in his smell – and the scent of fried rabbit. I paw at his pocket, and he laughs and digs out my dinner. Then I nestle under his arm. I wallow in his sweat, his odor, and the comfort of his bunk. I push aside the images of the cold, black bin as I curl close beside him.

Reveille blares.

Conroy crawls out of bed. I roll over and nuzzle under the covers, but Conroy finds me and stuffs me under his bunk.

"Stay here," he says. "And don't let anyone see you."

I start to yelp a protest – but then I remember the dark, sooty coal bin. So, I just whimper and back up under the cot with the dust bunnies – and dream of chasing real bunnies when we get off this boat.

When I wake, Conroy is still gone.

The dust tickles my nose, and I sneeze. I shake my head and sniff. Sweaty socks, smelling of Conroy, Sam, and the other boys. Before long, the socks lie shredded around me. Bored, I creep out and explore the cabin. One haversack smells of chocolate —I'll leave that one alone. At Sam's, though, I get whiffs of jerky. *Ah, yes! Beef!* I decide he won't mind sharing – just a little.

I rake and rake at the top of the haversack with my paw until it finally comes open. I wriggle my nose through the opening and find the prize. With my paws and teeth, I tear off the paper wrapping and bare my jerky treasure. *I'll just taste a little.* But with a gulp, all the delicious, meaty morsels disappear. I turn around and use my hind legs to kick the haversack and the paper remnants under the bunk so maybe he won't notice. Then I lay down for another nap.

The dim light in the cabin grows even darker by the time Conroy and his buddies come in and plop down on their bunks. Their haversacks remain stuffed under their cots, and my theft is undiscovered. Conroy scratches my ears as he and Sam talk about their day on deck and what they expect when we land.

"We'll have more training with the French infantry," says Conroy.

"I'm ready." Charlie peels off his shirt. "I'm ready to let Ole Fritz meet his first Americans!"

"Amen," agrees Conroy. "Right, Stubby old boy? We'll show those Germans the American way!" I lick his hand and turn my shoulder slightly so he can scratch it.

As Conroy settles back, I creep up beside him and nestle against his side, soaking in his odor. I drift off, dreaming of charging Ole Fritz and rounding him up and marching him back – and being a hero – just like my Conroy.

I wake up as Conroy laces his boots and stomps out of the bunkroom. I stick my nose out the door and sniff the sea air. The deck grows brighter as the sun inches up the sky. I sniff one way, turn and sniff in the other direction. *Fresh mouse.* It's time to hunt. I've been under that bunk for two days, creeping out only a little – and scooting back before the boys return. So far, no one except Conroy and his buddies know I am here.

Sometimes I've had to sneak out, though. After all, "nature calls." Peeing is easy. I just go aft to an empty corner and lift a leg. For the other, well -- let's just say Conroy has to do some daily shoveling – when he finds it, anyway.

Today I pad softly around a coil of ropes, sniffing for the mouse. The sun slips from behind a cloud and warms my fur. I stretch and yawn – then freeze.

"Halt!" barks the Captain. Instinctively, I tuck my tail between my legs.

Conroy rounds the deck as he hears the Captain's voice.

"What's this?" the Captain growls. My legs shake, but I hold still. I send Conroy a pleading look.

"That's Stubby, sir. Sort of a mascot, sir," stammers Conroy. He snaps to attention. I look up and inhale a deep breath. Remembering the Sergeant back at camp, I know what to do.

Pushing my shoulders back, I march a few steps in the Captain's direction. I stand straight, then sit on my rear legs, lifting my right paw over my eye. I raise my head and look straight at the Captain with my finest salute.

But the Captain holds his glare, his jaw tight.

I hold my pose as long as possible and try my best to smile. My fur stands up on my shoulders; my short tail shakes slightly, but I hold my stance.

After a long moment, the Captain relents.

"Keep 'em out of the way," he grunts. "And you had better clean up after him. I don't want to step in any of his mess." His eyes seem to pierce through my fur. "Or it's

Davy Jones' Locker for him."

I exhale. *Oh, yes. I'll stay out of the way.* Wherever Davy Jones' Locker is does not sound like a place I want to be. I hurry back to Conroy's side.

"Yes, sir," he answers.

Day and night, the ship chugs across the sea. With about twenty boats in our convoy, crossing the Atlantic takes about four weeks, or so Conroy says. At first, the chow is good – stewed rabbit! I like a rabbit! But then we have fish, and I'm not a fan of fish. And then we have rabbit again, and then for a change, we have rabbit and fish, till it comes out our ears. At last, one of my boys, Caleb, is ordered to the officer's cabin to work on the payroll, so he is able to sneak some beef, and he brings back a little for me. Otherwise, it's rabbit or fish – or occasionally *rat!*

The rats are just for me. The ship is full of them, stowaways themselves, probably, in grain bins or other crates. But they can't hide from my nose. *And I love me some fresh rat!* But as thankful as my boys are that I keep the vermin population down, they aren't too keen on my eating the rats. At first, I bring them a few – thinking they will be extra proud of me. Instead, they toss my catches over the side.

"Nasty rats!" they say.

What do you mean? I bark. *If you will just try one.*

One of the deckhands, called Yorkie, takes a liking to me. He's a skinny, black-haired fellow who smells of saltwater and dead fish and has an anchor tattooed on his forearm. Yorkie slips me bites of sweet cake from his dinner. When he does that, I let him scratch my ears.

One day he shows up with a pair of shiny metal discs.

"If you're gonna be a soldier, you need some dog tags," he says, "so I made these for you." He fastens the discs to my collar. I stiffen and look at Conroy. Conroy nods, and I relax.

Yorkie reads me the tags, "STUBBY 102ND INF 26TH DIV." He turns one tag toward Conroy. "See? There's your name, too – J.R. Conroy – around the edge."

Conroy turns to me with a chuckle. "Well, Stubby, old boy, looks like you've got your own honest-to-goodness dog tags." He pulls out a chain around his neck with two shiny discs attached. "Just like mine."

I shake my head and hear the ting as the discs collide. *Just like Conroy's.*

The soldiers were issued lifebelts when we first boarded the ship, and they are supposed to wear them at all times, even when they sleep. Boxy-looking contraptions are made of strips of cork with canvas straps that tie in front. They smell like saltwater and mold. They don't look comfortable, and I am glad I don't have to wear one. But they look like good chew toys. I decide to watch for one abandoned on deck. Conroy says that we are also assigned to lifeboats in case we are torpedoed by submarines.

For about a week, we have smooth sailing . . . then all heck breaks loose.

Boom!

"Hit the deck! Hit the deck!" The command echoes across the ship.

The ship's sirens blast. I hit the deck.

Boom! Another explosion rocks our ship, and then another! I skid across the deck and meet the sharp corner of a crate. *Yip!*

"Torpedoes! U-boats! To the lifeboats!" someone yells.

The crew scurries to the lifeboats assigned to them, with me close behind.

"Abandon ship! Abandon ship! I bark as loud as I can. *Where's my lifeboat?"* I run in circles. *"Abandon ship! Where's my lifeboat?"* The soldiers ignore my yelps.

"Conroy! Where's Conroy?" I bark. *"Where's my life vest! Conroy! Where's our lifeboat?"*

I am exhausted, and I huddle and shudder next to the ropes, whimpering like a puppy.

"C'mon, boy. I've got you!"

I leap and nearly knock Conroy down when I hear his voice.

"Attention!" The Captain's command booms above the din. "Stay on board. This is just a drill. Gunner practice. I repeat – this is just a drill. Back to your stations. We'll be docking soon."

"What? A drill? Was this just a drill? Just a drill my paw!" Such a drill could give a mutt a heart attack. I bark a few choice words toward the Captain.

I feel a sudden need to pee.

7

By the time we dock at Liverpool, I have my sea legs back and have calmed down. Conroy's buddies run what he calls "good interference" as he stuffs me, unnoticed, under his coat. He hoists his haversack and tromps off the ship.

Later we learn that our ship, the *USS Minnesota*, returns safely to the U.S. The ship Charlie came in on, though, (the *Missanabee*) is not so lucky. Hit by a torpedo, it sinks right outside the harbor.

"Dang!" says Charlie. "Torpedoed by a U-boat – with all our winter coats and boots, too. Down to 'Davey Jones's Locker'!"

I whine slightly. Davey Jones's Locker sounds like a scary place. I put my paw on Charlie's foot to comfort him. I'm glad that my coat is attached and can't be lost.

In Liverpool, we board our first British train. Packed in, elbow to elbow, Conroy and Charlie and Sam and Caleb sit on a bare wooden bench. I barely manage to squeeze under the seat. The constant rocking and clanging of metal against the rails make sleep impossible. The train car reeks of sweat, mildew, and soldiers I've never met. With no room to explore, I nestle as comfortably as possible on the hard floor. From behind the legs of the soldiers, I listen to them talk about the battles and weapons and the adventures ahead.

A shudder of sadness slips through me when I think about my Mama, but I shake it off. I'm a soldier dog, and I have a partner. I scoot closer to Conroy and lay my nose on his boot.

On our arrival in Southampton, we march to the town of Winchester. There we are assigned to a large, tented area. The tents are white and large enough for about forty boys to sleep. We all sleep on the floor this time. Of course, I am used to sleeping on the ground, but my boys groan as they toss and turn to find a comfortable spot. My nose is in a constant twitch from the mountain of smells from sweaty soldiers, boots, haversacks, and mud.

Like all humans, my boys stink. When they exhale, even if they don't speak, their breath shouts a barrage of all they've eaten that day and where they've been. That's how I really get to know them. Each boy has his own smell, and I memorize them all. Some stink more than others, like the lanky, tow-headed Caleb. He sweats a lot, even when it's cold out, and he mops his face on his sleeve. But sometimes, I can smell the bacon in his pocket, and I know he has brought me a treat. But my Conroy still smells the best.

The sleeping here may be challenging, but oh, the chow! Only two meals per day, but a feast compared to the ship grub. Conroy and Charlie put away hunks of bread, bacon, marmalade, and tea in the morning. Chunks of bread, marmalade, baked potato, bacon, and tea in the evening. *Me? Just bacon – give me your bacon!* Of course, they won't give me all of it, so I have to fill up with some bread, too. *If they would just throw in a rat once in a while.*

While we wait for a good day to cross the English Channel to France, we drill every day. We train with the French soldiers. They talk in a strange language, but I usually understand what they want from their tone of voice when they make commands. When they speak Conroy's language, they have a strange lilt in their voice. They smell different, too. I memorize their scents, more flowery than ours, and learn their uniforms and habits. Gradually, I pick up a few of their words, but mostly I look to Conroy to tell me what to do.

The Frenchmen call us the 'Doughboys,' which my boys think is funny.

"Maybe it's because we make more 'dough' than they do," Charlie suggests.

"Nah." Sam pulls out a knife and whittles on a stick. "It's 'cause we eat so many doughnuts." My ears perk up at that. I haven't seen a doughnut since we've been here.

"We'll be fighting with these French boys," Conroy tells me as he gives me a good rub down one evening. His eyes gleam. "Our American Army's not in this war yet, so we're the first Yankees over here."

He pulls in a deep breath and grins. I roll on my back and let him rub my belly.

We're the first, and we're gonna be heroes.

During the day, I drill for a couple of hours with my boys and then explore the territory. As I scratch around the flowers, I pick up the scents of the field mice, but they're good hiders. Before leaving, I lift my hind leg and mark the spot, so other animals will know I've been here and that I'll be back. As the sun warms my fur, I yawn and stretch out on the grass.

As the days pass, I listen to the conversations in English and French, and I begin to understand both languages better. I hear snatches of other human languages, too, but they are harder to understand. But I get pretty good at English and French. It's not that hard for a dog.

We dogs know humans better than they will ever know us. We're good watchers. We can tell what a human means just by watching his face and posture and hands. Combine this with the tone of their voices and the subtle scents they send out, and the meaning is pretty clear. I could talk back to them if I could just get my lips to move like theirs. But between my tail wags and my eyes and my bark, they usually understand me, too. Too bad we can't teach humans to sniff and follow their noses. You can tell a lot more from one's scent than his words. Scents don't lie.

We carry on this way for what seems like a month, but Conroy says it's been only a couple of weeks. Then a channel boat pulls into the dock, and we board her, bound for what he calls Le Havre, France.

Conroy calls the boat we're on the *Archangel*, but the *Archdemon* is more like it, if you ask me. Once again, we are packed in. The channel whitecaps, and cold waves spill over the deck. I slide from one side to the other, shivering, until Conroy sticks me under his coat, where I still shiver and whimper.

The boat rocks and crashes against the waves. Soldiers cling to the sides of the deck and hang over the rails, violently sick, vomiting their lunch. They shudder in misery and stick to the sides of the boat. The ship reeks with the sour stench of seasickness. I just know I am a goner as the boat does everything but go under.

Davey Jones's Locker, here we come!

Late in the evening, we pull into port. I stay tucked under Conroy's coat as he pulls his soaked duffel down the plank to solid ground. He lets me down, and I give my body a good shake and pick out a bush to pee.

But our day isn't over.

We march up the road in drizzling rain. As the heavy boots hit the puddles, mud splats on my fur. We trudge on. Just over a slight rise, the road dips suddenly. It winds down into old riverbed that is quickly filling with cold rain and mud. We hike up the steep hill on the other side and set up camp. The soldiers curse as they drive stakes and pull up the heavy canvas in the miserable rain. Finally, after chow of bread and beef stew, we huddle on the floor of the tents, the boys fully clothed, of course. Soon every mother's son -- and one tired puppy -- are dead to the world.

At last warm and dry next to Conroy's side, I dream of tracking a giant, gray rat. *I'm crouched and ready for the pounce . . .*

Shreeeeek! The blast of the bugle jolts me awake.

"What the hell!" yells Conroy, half asleep. "Doesn't he know it's two in the morning?"

"Is he drunk?" Charlie throws his arms over his ears and rolls over. "Somebody, grab that blasted bugle and smash it!"

But no, the call is official. I snap back into soldier mode and scurry around my boys, hurrying them to gear up. My Yankee Division boys sling on their packs, grab their rifles, and head down the hill, still half asleep but moving on. Our train is waiting. Shoulder to shoulder, the boys are jammed into grimy rail cars, and the train slowly pulls out. Once again, I ride, peering out behind Conroy's feet.

Posted to the inside walls of the rail cars are posters intended to spur on the soldiers. On one, a giant boot stomps a tiny fleeing German soldier. Conroy reads the bold banner across the top: STAMP OUT THE KAISER! My instant favorite poster shows battle flames shooting up behind a large, jagged rock. A lean and muscular German Shepherd stands atop the rock, proudly wearing a white harness emblazoned with a bright cross. *A canine hero!*

The boys point to the posters and jab each other and jibe about who'll be the bravest, the biggest hero. How any one of them can beat three of the Fritz.

I feel something grow bigger and stronger in my insides, like the strength to do mighty deeds. *Like the dog on the poster, I will be a brave warrior — a canine hero.*

The boxcars lumber on, and the rhythmic click-clack lulls some of the boys back to sleep; others chitter softly in anticipation as we near our destination.

My Yankee boys – and I – are bound for "The Western Front."

PART TWO - The Trenches

8

The rail car finally grinds to a stop. The minute it's open, I leap out the door – and take a tumble when I hit the slippery wet ground. I scramble up and dart to the nearest grassy patch. Ignoring the tall blades tickling my belly, I lift my rear leg, close my eyes, and pee – *ah...relief*. A couple of my boys find some bushes nearby and relieve themselves, too. Then the boys hoist their haversacks, and we march.

We tromp for hours down muddy roads. The bellicose bragging on the train dwindles to muttering as we trudge on. We march. And we march. And we march. My short legs grow achy, but I keep up. We march all day long, miles and miles, it seems to me.

Other divisions join us, and I see other working animals on our road. Horses, mules, and oxen strain at pulling artillery and ammunition through the muck. Some pull supply wagons or camp kitchens. Calvary horses kick up mud as they trot past. Occasionally another dog trots alongside the soldiers. I try to dash over and make friends.

"Stubby, heel!" Conroy's command is sudden and

fierce. I tuck tail and scoot immediately back in line with my boys and resume the march.

Occasionally, we do get out of line, though. Conroy becomes what he calls a 'dispatch rider,' which means he sometimes rides a horse (a horse that I'm not allowed to taunt) and delivers messages between command posts. On these missions, I get to trot alongside as we take shortcut trails through the countryside. We get to see some of the small villages this way.

On one of these trips, we see American soldiers shoveling away a giant pile of manure from beside a farm shed. I race over and sniff the scat. Horse . . . and goat! *Now, why would humans want to move that?*

"You're wasting your time. The farmers will just pile it back." Conroy calls to the soldiers as he rides up next to the house. "I've seen it several times down the road.

"Yeah? Well, we've got to sleep here tonight," one of them answers. "And we don't want to smell it all night." He takes his shovel and knocks manure from his boot. Then he turns and goes back to shoveling.

With a shrug, Conroy calls me back, and we continue our trip.

Soon I spot a rabbit and charge the bush.

"Stubby, no! Get back here." Conroy's voice is harsh.

What's his problem? Dogs are supposed to chase squirrels and rabbits and deer. Sometimes I don't understand humans.

But I obey. At first, I hang my head and look dejected, but Conroy ignores me and rides on. So, I just concentrate on keeping up and listening and smelling for danger. Conroy is my partner, and it's my job to follow him. At the end of the day, he gives me a brisk rubbing all over and tells me, "Good boy." I like that.

After each mission, we fall back into formation and march with our other boys.

The rains continue, and the cold wind comes. My boys slog through the slippery yellow mud. I try to keep up, pulling my paws out of the sucking muck and sneezing mud pellets out my nose. But I don't complain. My boys are wet and cold. Their boastful chattering from before sinks to groans, but they tromp on, steadfast and determined. And so do I, thankful for my warm coat that sheds the water and keeps me warm. Rations grow scanty, but Conroy still shares his with me.

When night falls, we find shelter in leaky lofts or empty stables. The cold dampness mixes with the scents of the cows or horses and their hay and manure. I breathe deep, taking them in. Exhausted from the march, I curl up on a hay bale next to Conroy and keep him warm.

This war is not so hard, I decide. *A little wet and cold, but mostly just marching and drilling.* I close my eyes with images of a brave canine warrior.

The screech of the bugle shatters the air all too soon, and we repeat our day of marching. As we do the next day – and the next day – and the next.

One night, I get my boys settled in a barn and venture into the woods. I spot a rabbit at the edge of an orchard and take off, but I am no match. It darts into a thicket of briars and disappears. It's not worth the scratches to pursue it.

I draw in the clean, woodsy odors and pull in another -- scent sweet and tangy – like apples ripening.

Plop! I spin around.

Plop! I creep toward the sound. A large, dark, two-legged form stretches up into a tree and shakes the branches.

Plop! Plop! Plop! Apples hit the ground. The man untucks his shirttail and loads the apples into his shirt basket. Then he ducks low and sprints off toward camp. As he passes, I catch a faint whiff of chocolate. *Charlie!* I bound off after him.

"Hey, look what I found!" Charlie calls to Conroy and the others as he lets his bounty roll down into a trough.

"All right! Apples!" Sam jumps up, grabs an apple, and shines it across his shirt. The apple crunches and spews juice as he bites in. He cocks his half-grin.

"Wait a minute." Conroy glances at the others. "I thought we had orders to leave the farm produce alone."

"Ahh, they won't miss a few," Charlie mumbles, his mouth full. The juice dribbles down his chin.

"Well, just don't make it a habit." Conroy tries to sound stern, but he grabs an apple for himself.

I can't help but drool. *I wish I liked apples!* I settle in beside Conroy and rest my head on my paws.

One day, our march is interrupted by a convoy of trucks rolling in.

"Attention!" calls the Sergeant. My boys jump to a stand as the lead truck grinds to a halt. I slip behind Conroy's legs and peer through. Two officers in crisp, clean uniforms step from the truck. One is tall and tanned, with bright-colored patches across his chest. From beneath thick, dark brows, stern eyes cross the line of soldiers. A heavy bush grows over his upper lip.

"Salute!" commands the Sergeant. The lines of soldiers snap in unison. The officer returns the salute. The Sergeant turns back to the newcomers. "Colonel Parker, sir!" He salutes the officer.

And I know what to do. I dart from behind Conroy's legs and plant my own legs in front of the officer.

"Stubby, back here!" Conroy whisper-commands. But I ignore him.

With my back erect, I sit and rear on my haunches. I slowly raise my right paw over my eye, keeping my look steady on the officer's face.

"What's this?" snaps the Colonel.

Conroy steps forward. "He's mine, sir. That's um, that's Stubby, sir." The officer looks from me to Conroy to the Sergeant.

"Mascot, sir," says the Sergeant, still in salute.

"Smart dog." The Colonel's eyes smile slightly. "At ease, soldiers."

As the officers turn to go, I give a couple of short barks in answer.

"Stubby, hush!" orders Conroy. "Come here, Stubby." Conroy sounds suddenly tense.

Colonel Parker turns back and eyes me.

"That may be the first time a soldier's talked back to me." He pauses for a long moment. I feel Conroy's muscles knot up. "And gotten away with it." He chuckles and turns back to the officers.

Conroy exhales. My heart swells. *I like to make Conroy proud.*

The icy rain continues, and the puddles get deeper as we resume our march to the mountains. As we near the front line, the path grows more dangerous with gaping holes from recent shelling. The holes fill with rain, and at dusk, it's easy to mistake a hole for solid ground. More than one soldier suddenly finds himself up to his knees in a puddle, with mud pouring into his already wet boots. I watch and make sure I skirt around the puddles. Knee-deep on a soldier is over my head!

The air gets colder every day. Rain turns to sleet. Some of the boys suffer frozen feet and hands, especially those who'd arrived on the *Missanabee* with Charlie. When it went down, they lost their winter clothes and gloves.

Galen, one of my boys from that ship, salvages a couple of bread sacks to wrap his feet against the cold. When we stop for chow, I spot him rubbing his feet. I go over, make a couple of circles, and lie down across his feet to help thaw some feeling back in his toes before we start marching again. As his feet warm up, he rubs my back.

Some of the others, rewrapping their feet in rags and sacks, send me wishful looks for some of my heat.

9

When we finally stop and make camp, Conroy announces the town: "*Chemin des Dames.*"

At base camp, a short, squat fellow with a pale face and uneasy eyes approaches the boys. He chews a straw as he speaks.

"I'm Private Girard. You're to follow me." Girard smacks of sausage and mustard and *mischief*. Humans can fool each other with smiles and happy faces, but they can rarely fool us. Their scents tell all.

My neck fur stands up; I emit a low growl. "Easy, boy," whispers Conroy. I keep silent but stay on alert as I trot beside Conroy.

We follow Girard, slogging through the mud. The path slants downward. It grows darker. We are entering the trenches. We trudge through what Girard calls the communication trenches and the support trenches before heading for the front line.

Mud... Pee... Rats... and a hundred new scents tickle my nose, but there is no time to sort them out. I trot briskly to keep up with Conroy.

The trench twists or turns every few yards, crossed by occasional other trenches, until it forms a maze of intersecting ditches. The rows of tracks snake and zigzag across huge fields. As we wind through, my ears twitch, alert.

"Why all the twists?" asks Conroy.

"Huh. So Ol' Fritz can't get a straight shot at all of us at once," grunts Girard.

Fritz. Huns. Kaiser. Boche. All the names Conroy and my boys call the enemy. *Why don't they just call them Germans?*

My boys tromp through the wet trenches, some trenches deep enough for them to stand up in; others smaller so the boys have to duck and crawl through them. Occasionally, a camouflaged tunnel leads out from the side to an underground command barracks.

Private Girard stops at one of the dugout rooms. A sentry and two runners crouch on the ground at the doorway. One of the runners nods to Girard, disappears into the dugout, returns quickly, and motions us in.

The dim underground room looks big enough for two of my boys to lie in it end to end. Plank floors, with dirt walls and dirt ceilings propped up with more planks. Bunks line the walls, and a table sits in the middle. Amid the dampness wafts the scent of kerosene. At the table sit three soldiers, all with stripes across their shirts.

I start to dart in, but Conroy whisper-calls me back. He shoots me a look that says *Quiet!*

"Private Girard reporting with the Americans, sir." Girard salutes the officer.

"Good to have you, boys. I'm Colonel Isbel. Captain Rous will take you to your stations."

Captain Rous stands. He is tall and thin, his elbows jutting sharply in his jacket when he salutes. He tilts his head up, cocky, like a poodle I knew back home. I sniff cigarettes and cheese. Under his short-cropped hair the color of hay, his eyes are sharp.

"Let's go, boys," says Captain Rous. Then he eyes me, like a hawk eyeing a little wren. "What's that dog doing here?" I sit still as a rock by Conroy's leg. My heart thumps faster.

"That's Soldier Stubby." Conroy jumps to explain. "He's sort of our mascot."

"Hmmph." The Captain shoots a look at the Colonel and back at me.

I stand straight and tall. *Mascot must mean hero.* I pose, ready to salute, my pulse still racing. But Conroy steps his foot in front of me. The Captain shoots his look back toward Conroy.

We stand silent for a moment.

"See that he doesn't get in the way."

"Yes, sir." Conroy click-clicks his mouth for me, and we follow the Captain out.

We finally arrive at our station, the frontline trench — the one closest to the enemy. Here workers are shoveling mud out of channels and putting down planks for the soldiers to walk on. Ladders lead into and out of the trenches on the sides facing the fighting.

"Watch your step on the duckboards," warns the Captain.

Duckboards? Ducks? I sniff the air. Nothing. I spin my head to the right. *No ducks.* I spin to the left. *No ducks.*

Soldiers shovel sand into bags and build up the walls on the front and back of the trench. They twist and stack the bags along the top, leaving peepholes for the sentries to watch through the night.

"Why stack them on the back?" Sam asks one of the

men.

"To keep Fritz's shrapnel from blowing back on us." The soldier doesn't break stride but keeps refilling the bags as he answers. The soldiers taking a rest, reach out grimy hands to pet me. They smell like sweat and gunpowder and dirt.

I keep alert and take mental notes. It will be up to me to keep my boys safe.

"If you want to risk getting shot, stick your head over the parapet," Private Girard cocks one eyebrow as he chews his straw. "It's safer to use the peepholes. But you can see our barbed wire entanglements and a field pocked with shell holes. Then there's the German's barbed wire, and then their trenches."

Sam eyes the parapet. I dart over and tug his pant leg, but he stretches his neck over the top. Almost instantly, the air barks and whizzes and thuds behind the back wall. Dirt and metal shards spray over the trench and rain down on the ducking boys. I jump over to Conroy's feet and shake off the dirt. *Yeah, that's why I'm shaking. Not scared. Not me, nope. Heroes aren't afraid. Uh uh. Just gotta shake off some dirt.*

I catch a glimpse of Girard's smirk.

"Got it." Sam brushes off his jacket and spits dirt as he offers his half-grin. "Won't do that again."

Right, Sam. Keep your head down. I don't like that raining dirt!

When evening comes, the boys hunker down on the driest boards to sleep. They sleep in snatches amid the filth of standing water, mud, and garbage. I sniff, then sneeze out the dank odors of decay and mildew and – pee.

"So, um. Where we go when we gotta go?" Sam evidently smells it, too.

"Find you a bucket," mutters the Captain.

I shake my head and wipe my nose. *Yeah, I can smell the buckets.* Again, I'm thankful to be a dog where all I need is an empty stretch of trench.

"Watch out, bud!" barks one soldier. Foul-smelling liquid sloshes out of his bucket as he winds through our group. I hop to the side just in time.

Buckets spill and slosh onto the boards. My boys jump back. In addition to the pee smell, the men who have been here for a while reek from lack of baths or change of clothes.

Sometimes a sharp nose isn't that much of a blessing.

Here in the trenches, my boys fight the enemy, and here they fight the lice. Sam and the Southern boys call the lice "cooties," which makes the Yankees laugh, but these cooties are no laughing matter. The soldiers find cooties in their clothes, cooties in their hair, and cooties in their gear. The soldiers scratch like they have fleas, and the scratches turn into sores. In the filth of the trench, the sores fester with infection. *Kind of like the mange.*

One of the soldiers is having a fit of scratching when we round a twist in the trench.

"Hey! What's that cur doing in here?" he growls. "Don't we got enough fleas? Get that fleabag outta here!" He rips off his shirt and gives it a vicious shake.

The fellow smells bitter. His face is young and smooth, round, and un-whiskered, but under his blond curly hair, his eyebrows pinch together in a scowl.

"What ya lookin' at?" He shoots angry words at me, then whips around, still shaking his shirt. I see thin whelps of scars across his back. He jerks back around and pops his shirt in the air toward me. His jaw and fists are clenched tight. His voice makes my tail sink.

"I said, get that mongrel out of here!"

Mongrel? I may be a mix, but I'm no mongrel! I narrow my eyes and emit a low growl. The hair on my neck stiffens.

"Easy, buddy." Conroy speaks to me, but I think he means both of us.

"Enough, Private Moore!" The Captain barks. "Now, back to your work."

Conroy shoos me on around the next twist. *Doesn't he know that dogs don't carry lice?* I'm still seething at the man's insult. *Maybe I should just shorten his nose a little and teach him a thing or two.*

"Ignore Billy back there," the Captain tells Conroy when we're around the next bend. "I don't know what his problem is, but he came here with a chip on his shoulder."

Some of the cootie-infested men do look miserable, though. I hope my boys don't get cooties.

I feel a sudden compulsion to scratch my neck.

If they do, will they blame me, too?

10

In the trenches, I get to know my Yankee boys like family. I snuggle among their feet to keep them warm as I listen to their stories about family and girlfriends back home. I learn which boys are brave (like my Conroy), who are just blustering, and who are really scared. With the scared ones, I nuzzle and yip quiet words of comfort. I learn their moods, who likes to laugh, and who wants to be quiet. Some of the quiet ones, like Sam, scratch on paper at night. (A *diary*, Conroy calls it one night when I stick my nose up under Sam's arm so I can see.) I even learn the boys' favorite foods. (Conroy's are beef and potatoes.)

Some nights as I lie in the darkness, their talking dims to mumbling, and images of the day drift through my head -- the foods I have eaten, the rats I have chased. Every so often, through the mumbling, I hear "Stubby," and my ears perk up. But the boys just move on, talking about other things, and I settle back down. Conroy scratches my ears while he talks, or I curl up with my head on his boots. He is my partner. I like the same people he likes, and he likes these boys. So, these boys are my boys, and it's my job to protect them.

After all, I'm better equipped.

A human's nose is almost useless. They can't smell anything until it's literally under their noses. In the dark, they can't make out one person from another. But I know the scent of each of my boys. I can smell their moods, what they've eaten, and where they've been. And I can sense when a stranger comes by without even looking up.

But sometimes, a keen nose can be a curse.

The trench is a cacophony of odors, aside from the stench of the latrines. Added to the poop and pee odors are the smells of rotting sandbags, explosives, gun smoke, and poison gas. Some of these odors, like the gun smoke, I recognize right away. The fumes of gun powder taste bitter on my tongue. Others, like the poison gas and explosives and infection, I learn on the job.

The vile, overwhelming stench of all this filth assaults my sensitive nose, but I stay with my boys. I use my nose to protect them. My job is important, and I like that.

As my group of Dough Boys trudges deeper in the trench, another battle-worn troop staggers off, many suffering from coughs and colds. The stench of infection wafts as they pass.

"They look rough." Charlie steps to the side to give them room.

"Yeah," says Captain. "Some of 'em got trench fever from the lice. Some of 'em trench foot from the mud, and some got trench mouth. A trench is a good place to get sick. With all this wet and cold and vermin, it's a wonder we're not all sick."

I give a quick bark. *Not my boys. Not sick. I'll take care of them.*

One familiar and distinct scent creeps through the damp, putrid smells of trench filth: *Rats*. Trench rats. Rats are everywhere and eat anything and everything.

The soldiers seal up and hide their chow at night as best they can, but an army of vermin freely scamper and feed on any forgotten leftovers. They gnaw holes in the haversacks and eat any rations they can find.

"Dang rats grow big as cats down here," mutters an old, ragged soldier. He hocks a loogie and spits skillfully between his feet. "Dang rats will run right over your face if you don't keep it covered when you sleep."

Rats as big as a cat? I snap to attention. *I am ready. Bring 'em on. Soldier Stubby is on duty.*

"We tried drenching the place with creosote once," says a straggly-looking boy as he picks at an acne sore. "It almost suffocated us, but it didn't stop them. They came pattering down the steps the usual time, stopped a moment, sneezed, then got to work gnawing on our sacks."

Killing rats becomes my number one job in the trench. And I am good at it. Their gnawing wakes me up, and they're easy to spot – their eyes gleaming green in the dark. After I catch a few and crunch their heads, the others are not so brazen around my boys. And that makes my boys happy. They reward me with bits of bacon from their chow.

Bacon, aah yes. The rewards of a soldier.

W-h-e -e -e, Boom!

The flashes and whines and pops and rumbles of the enemy guns become routine. At first, I howl and dart around, but Conroy holds me and rubs me and whispers to me. Soon I adjust to the blasts and exploding earth. Twice, the booms blow me off my feet, but I roll, scramble to a stand, and shake off the dirt. After the bursting shells, we duck and dodge the dirt that the falling shrapnel kicks up.

As I stand by Conroy at dawn, some whizz-bangs skim the top of the trench. The sandbag above me bursts open. I choke, half-blind, and paw at my eyes. The soldier to my right shrieks and falls back into the trench, grabbing his face. I drop for cover next to him -- shaking. I nuzzle my nose under his arms, and he drops one hand from his face to my neck. I look up at his round, dough-white face smeared with tears and blood oozing from the side of his head. *Caleb!*

I lick his nose, and he manages a chuckle.

"It's okay, fellow. Anybody with half a brain would be a little scared."

My chest quivers. My back shakes. My heart pounds. But I've got to get help!

More shells explode overhead. In the din of noise, I hear Conroy's call. "Stubby!"

I wriggle loose and belly-crawl over to Conroy. He squeezes me and brushes the sand from my head, but I squirm out of his hands and tug at his leg. With a short yip, I crawl back to Caleb. Blood rolls down his face under his hands. I whimper encouragement as Conroy crawls over behind me.

"Come on, buddy. We'll get you out of here" Conroy grabs a rag and presses it to Caleb's face. Blood seeps out from the bandage, smelling sweet and metallic. Conroy presses harder.

"Hang in there, Caleb. You're going to be all right. Just hold this over that eye and come with me."

Conroy grabs Caleb under the arm and pulls him up. I follow as he threads Caleb through the trench and sets him down at the medic station. Then he reaches down and scratches my ear.

"Good boy, Stubby. You're a good soldier."

I roll my head and let him scratch the other ear. At his touch, I quit shaking.

Gradually, I grow used to our days and nights in the trenches. The thunder in my ears starts to seem normal. After each shell blast, I scamper around to check on my boys. If one of them is injured, I *yelp!* for the Medic.

If Ole Fritz isn't pounding us with shells, we begin our mornings with "Stand To" about an hour before sunrise. That's when the boys ready their weapons. Dawn raids by the Fritz are common, but our boys are ready with bayonets attached to their rifles.

As daylight breaks, our own shells pound the enemy trenches.

"The Morning Hate," Conroy explains one morning as he tosses me a biscuit from his plate. I catch it mid-air. "Some say it tests our weapons, but I think it just helps the guys get rid of some stress from a night in the trench." I wag my tail to let him know I am listening. I keep my eye on a scrap of bacon still on his plate. My tongue darts out when he's not looking and laps it into my mouth.

The mess boys pass along buckets of steaming coffee with the morning chow. After breakfast, the boys face inspection by the commanding officer; then, they set to chores repairing sandbags, duckboards, and latrines.

In the afternoon, unless we are in battle, some boys

take turns as guards. Others try to catch up on sleep, write letters, or even play cards. Sam scratches in his diary. But we always keep our heads down, out of sight of shells and shrapnel.

Days stretch long in the trench. The boys are unshaven and filthy, their uniforms and boots crusted over with mud. Conroy takes a tin of water to wash off his rifle and then uses his bayonet to scrape the excess mud from his shoes. He runs his hands through his matted hair, gives up, and just covers it up with his cap. Just a good shake is all the cleaning I need, or maybe to bite off chunks of mud that stick to my paws. Then I'm ready to go.

Evening comes, and the trenches come to life. The whine and *boom* of frequent whiz-bangs keep us alert, their concussion blowing out our dim candles. When possible, the boys stand for their second "Stand-To" of the day. Some men are sent to the rear for extra food and ammunition. Some others stand guard. Guard duty is in two-hour shifts, but after days in the trenches, some men fight to stay awake even for two hours.

If I see one of my boys dozing off, I nip their ankles. Conroy says that being caught asleep at his post will earn him death by firing squad, so I keep all my boys awake.

Except for Billy. If his eyes close, I nudge his leg and jump back. He wakes with a snarl and kicks out – like he's aiming for me or something. Why does he hate dogs? *Or is it just me?*

Rain and storms pound us nearly every day. Nothing seems to dry out, and my boys are constantly sneezing and coughing from the damp coldness.

As the boys huddle around a tiny fire one evening, Giraud lights a cigarette and offers one to Conroy.

"No thanks," answers Conroy. "I never learned to

like those things."

"Sitting out in this cold mess, and you don't smoke fags? I just don't know about you," Giraud takes a long drag on his cigarette. The end glows as he sucks in and then goes dark again as he blows his smoke toward me. I cough and crawl behind Conroy's legs.

"What's there to know." Conroy stares into the fire. "Smoker or not, you're either a good soldier or a bad soldier. The good one might save your life, and the other one will get you killed. And the Fritz don't care what kind you are."

"Did you always want to be a soldier?" Giraud takes another draw, and the end again turns bright.

Conroy sits silently for a minute. I feel his heart pumping and blood rushing, and I know he's thinking about his home, especially his sisters. He talks about them a lot.

"Not really." Conroy pokes a stick in the fire, and it blazes up a little. "My dad died when I was little, and my mom just a few years ago. My sisters are grown now, and I was ready to do something else. Then the President put out the call. I really signed up to be a mounted scout." His boots make a sucking sound as he shifts his position. "I certainly wasn't counting on these lovely trenches." I turn and put my head on his boot.

"I didn't have a lot of choices," says Giraud. "My family was dirt poor – hardly a potato in the pot or a franc in the pocket. I saw this as a chance for three hot meals a day and a warm place to sleep." He drags on the cigarette again and blows the smoke in little rings above his head. He gestures around their muddy abode. "Boy, did I get fooled!"

"Achoo!"

I jump up, awake. I must have dozed off.

"Achoo!"

"Achoo!"

"Achoo!"

I skirt around until I find the source of the sneeze – Old Jeb – a skinny, knotty-looking soldier who is having a fit of sneezing. Stringy, iron-gray hair sticks out from under his cap and shakes with each sneeze.

"Shhh!" grumbles a soldier trying to nap. "Keep it down over there."

Old Jeb tries, but he can't stop. Wisps of wiry hair jut out in all directions in a mix of bed head and helmet hair. It flops back and forth with each sneeze.

"Achoo!"

He sneezes and sneezes and sneezes. He holds his breath, pinches his nose, and snorts water. Nothing helps. He squeezes his nose AND holds his breath while Conroy counts . . . twenty-six, twenty-seven, twenty-eight…

"Achoo!"

A massive sneeze explodes out of Old Jeb's mouth.

"Oh, hell!" he half-whispers a yell. "My teeth! I lost my teeth!"

Teeth? Can teeth come out? I quickly slide my tongue over my canines. *Still there. Good.*

Conroy fumbles among the sandbags but finds nothing. A flash bursts across the sky as a shell arcs overhead. In the light, I spot the orphaned teeth a few feet out from the trench. When the flash fades, I slowly belly-crawl over to the choppers and grab them in my mouth. They feel smooth and hard like one of the boys' spoons. I hurry back and drop the teeth at Old Jeb's feet.

"Why, thank ye' feller." Old Jeb chuckles as he scratches my head. Then he pours water from his canteen over his teeth and sticks them back in his mouth.

His sneezes are gone. He stands there, half grinning, his false teeth staring at me.

"We'd better get back to camp and get some rest," says Conroy when our watch is over. "Tomorrow night, we go out to No Man's Land."

In No Man's Land, I'll need my nose and my next-best weapon – my ears.

STUBBY'S WAR

11

The camp is warm and dry compared to the cold, wet trenches. Conroy heats a bucket of water, bathes, and changes his clothes. He cleans his rifle. I fetch his bayonet, and he snaps it on.

"Now we're ready. Let's get some shut-eye," Conroy mumbles as he pulls his wool blanket over his shoulders. I curl up under his cot, but our rest is fleeting.

Conroy stirs on his bunk around midnight, and I shoot up straight.

"It's time, old boy. Time for No Man's Land." He shakes the bunk next to him. "Up and at 'em, Sam!"

Conroy and Sam pull strange black coveralls over their uniforms.

"These are our 'crawling suits,' Stubby," Sam explains. "Black, so they can't see us. And we're gonna be crawling around low like you."

"Yeah, but the Fritz may be out there, too. In his

own camouflage." Conroy pulls on a black mask and shapeless black hood. I bark and snap to attention, growling low.

From under his hood, I hear Conroy's chuckle. "It's still me, ole boy." I take a step back, but Conroy's hand reaches out and tousles my neck fur. "It's still me." His black hood turns toward another hooded figure standing where Sam used to be. "You remember what to do if we hear 'em?"

"Yep." Sam's voice comes from under the hood. "If we hear them, we play dead . . . and pray."

Play dead? I can do that. And they'll have my keen ears and nose out there to watch out for the enemy "crawlers."

Their Corporal nods in satisfaction when Conroy and Sam join the other two in the scouting mission.

"With any luck, we'll bring home the bacon tonight," he says.

Bacon? Where? My drool must be dribbling out because Conroy laughs.

"Come on, boy." He sounds confident, but I sense his heart pounding.

At the start, all is quiet as we climb out of our front trench. My ears tip forward, focusing on every sound and movement. We pick our way, silent as cats, through the debris of the day's fighting.

No Man's Land is the desolate wasteland between the two enemies' trenches, pitted with shell holes, and blasted and seared with the day's barrage of shells and falling shrapnel.

"Now, boys," says the Corporal in a low voice. "Remember to . . . Drop!"

His command shoots through the dark as the boys flatten on the ground. I drop beside Conroy, motionless.

Overhead, a star shell arcs in a flash of greenish light.

We lie still, playing dead. After the light fades, we rise and, like shadows, creep forward again. The sky lights up again.

"Drop!" A shell whistles overhead. We flatten again. *Boom!* It splits the earth to our right. Dirt rains over my coat. I pinch my eyes shut until it stops falling.

My ears stay alert; I sniff for danger. Dirt, gunpowder, boots, blood, death. I sort the scents as I guide my boys forward.

The moon clouds over, and night falls almost pitch black. This helps avoid detection, but it makes it difficult for my boys to navigate the shell-pocked rubble. But I can see, so I lead the way. *To the enemy barbed wire fence*, Conroy had said. *We need to get there and snip holes so our soldiers can slip through on tomorrow's assault.*

"Gee," whispers Sam. "I never saw a night so dark. You could cut it with a knife."

"Just hope that's the only thing gets cut tonight," mutters the Corporal.

"Follow me," says Conroy. "Stubby will get us there."

The Captain or the Corporal may bark the orders, but Conroy is my human and my pack leader. I look up to him. He signals and I lead the group forward.

We soon reach a patch of bushes near some ghastly naked trees. With their bark burnt off from shell fire, they stretch up like skeletons in the night sky. The boys crouch near them and listen for enemy patrols out on their own mission, much like ours.

But it's my ears they depend on. I pity the humans who can't hear anything until it's right in front of them, sometimes not even then. My ears work with my nose. As smells drift through my nostrils, I lean to my left, then to my right.

From the scent and the sound, I get a pretty good

picture of what's ahead long before it can get to me.

My boys follow me.

The night remains silent, and we creep on. As we draw near the enemy wire fence, the boys drop to hands and knees and then to a belly crawl, their hands stretched and scouting before them. I'm surrounded by blood and dirt and decaying flesh – the smell of death.

"Dang it!" mutters Sam, recoiling suddenly as his hand discovers a dead corpse. I nudge Sam around, and he crawls past the body.

I give a soft yip when my nose finally touches the cold, sharp metal of the fence.

"Here," Conroy signals to the others in a quick whisper. Sam crawls up with the wire cutters.

An approaching scent alerts me. My ears grow stiff, focusing on a sound – a near-silent step.

"Rrrr," I growl, a low, stealthful warning. Then the boys hear it . . . a faint footfall on the duckboards.

The boys flatten like lifeless shadows.

We wait. Several yards away, we spot a German sentry. He stops -- lights a cigarette. The red tip glows as he draws in the smoke and then exhales. He waits. Draws in again. Exhales. After a long moment, he turns and saunters back.

We lie silent for several more minutes. An enemy patrol could be lying nearby, as silent themselves and as watchful, but my nose tells me we are alone. I nudge Conroy.

"Let's do it," Conroy whispers to the others. He holds the wire between the barbs, and Sam snips it. They time their snips to the distant artillery fire to drown out any sounds of their cutting. After they cut enough to make gaps for the soldiers to slip through, they mark the areas with small white rags so our boys can find the holes in tomorrow's attack.

My boys are getting clever.

On bellies again, the boys crawl back, like earthworms. Once again, I scout the way. I stiffen and give a low, warning growl as we near the straggly trees. My boys freeze, lifeless. My eyes search through the dark shapes. No movement. Silence.

But I can smell the danger. I remain statue-still and watch. Then, a slender spear-like point rises above the hedge, followed more slowly by the growing figure -- of a German helmet.

Behind me, I hear Conroy slowly pull his rifle forward. The German sentry stands up straight. His head turns from side to side. Evidently convinced that what he has heard is nothing, he stoops to pick up his rifle.

Like a cat, Conroy springs from his shadow and butts the sentry with the stock of his gun. *Whack*! The German falls, and Conroy tightens his bayonet against German's throat to stifle any cry. Sam joins him and grabs the German's rifle. I clamp down on the soldier's ankle. With a quick uppercut from Sam, the sentry is laid unconscious on the ground.

Quickly Conroy and Sam tie the sentry's hands with his own belt and tie a gag across his mouth. Together, they grab him under the shoulders and drag their captive back to our comrades.

"Hey, does this count as our bacon?" whispers Conroy with a chuckle.

Bacon? My drool drips.

"Well done," says the Corporal. "But we're not out of the woods yet."

Dragging the sentry is easier with four of them, and we carefully make our way back to our own trench. The boys pick up the captive and carry him to our commander. They prop him under a tree, and I stand guard.

"Rrrr," I growl as the Fritz moans and begins to wake. He smells of vinegar and pork and cigarettes – and fear? I study his face. He looks down with wide, round eyes. *He's just a boy – like my boys. But he's a Fritz – the enemy, right? But just a boy.*

"Rrrr," I stand alert.

Conroy whistles for me, and we trudge back. We tromp the puddle-pocked dirt road for about an hour before meeting the train tracks back to camp.

Without washing up, the boys throw down their rifles and line up for chow: mashed potatoes, beefsteak, and gravy. *Ah . . . beef!* I trot back to our bunk with my belly full while Conroy makes his report.

Down the row of bunks sits Billy, his naked, scarred back to me. He shakes out his shirt, cursing the cooties. Using the tiny flame of his cigarette lighter, he sizzles the buggers along the seams. He takes his boot knife, scrapes the charred bodies from the crevices, and then throws the shirt on the cot. Extending his arm, he takes the knife and flicks tiny cuts in the flesh along the inside. *Is he cutting out cooties?*

Conroy's and Sam's boots crunch in the gravel, and Billy snaps his knife shut and quickly slips his arms in his shirt sleeves. Without a word, he slides down on the thin mattress, his face still to the wall.

"That was a helluva night," says Sam.

"Yeah." Conroy falls back on his bunk. "Let's get some rest. Tomorrow, we go again."

Underneath the bunk, satisfaction curls through me. This mission is new, and I know it is important. We caught an enemy, and I helped. But as I try to settle in, the boy's face drifts through my mind and mingles with Billy's. I see the boy's arms bound with his belt, but I picture Billy's arms, flecked red under his shirt.

Just a boy.

STUBBY'S WAR

12

Days and nights pass, and we hunker down in the pouring rain. Mud seeps through the duckboards, and my boys slog through in sodden uniforms. I scramble along the edges, trying to avoid the deepest parts. Fritz is also hunkered down in his trenches, but he still rains down the shells to keep us alert.

Supply trucks get stuck in the sludge of roads, rations grow slim, and our soup grows thinner. I crawl along the stretch, encouraging my boys, who share an extra morsel here and there when they can. Many soldiers fall sick, their coughing and hacking mixing with the pops of shells and plops of heavy rain. Their sickness I can't help. So far, my Conroy has stayed well.

Scents of fever and infection wind through the trench. I find Galen curled up in a ball, shivering. His eyes are closed, his face pale under streams of rain. I yelp an alert and press next to his side, keeping him warm. Conroy spots me and calls for the medics.

"Influenza," says the Medic as they load Galen onto a stretcher. "Between frostbite and influenza, it seems like it's getting as many of our boys as the Germans." They carry Galen out, and my patrol resumes.

Stay strong, I yip to my boys. *The weather will break. Stay strong.*

And at last, the rain slackens.

On a rare, moonlit night without rain, my boys sleep in the trench, exhausted; Sam snores like a freight train. I catch a few winks' sleep, my chin resting on Conroy's leg stretched across the duckboard.

A long, low whine wakes me, followed by a faint scraping, like a can scuttling across pebbles. A foreign smell, acrid and burning, drifts over the trench. I shoot to attention. *Grrrr.* The hair bristles down my back.

Fear ripples down my spine. I bark loud and sharp!

Wake up, Boys! Wake up! Danger's afoot!

Woof! I bark! I yelp! I pounce on Conroy, yelping in his ear.

Conroy stirs, sniffs the air, and starts yelling.

"Gas! Get the masks! Gas! Wake up! Gas!"

The boys scramble up and grab the masks.

Conroy tries to hold a mask over my nose, but it doesn't fit. The gas seeps into my nostrils.

I can't breathe. I stagger back. I stumble. I choke and teeter. As if in slow motion, I watch the ground coming closer.

My eyes burn. I squeeze them shut
My lungs are closing.
I can't breathe!

Terror rips through me.

Then I'm being lifted. My airways burn, and my insides shake. I hold my breath. I'm too scared to breathe.

The touch on my skin is familiar, but still, I quiver. *Help me!*

"Hang in there, Stubby. I've got you." Conroy's voice cracks through the fog.

Half-conscious, I feel a rhythmic lope. Conroy is running, cradling me against his chest.

As he runs, I slip off into the blackness. I wake and still feel his lopes.

We stop. A tent door flaps open.

"Help me!" Conroy calls between coughs and gasps. All is black.

Fire's in my eyes. Fire's in my nose. Fire's in my throat. I can't breathe!

I'm drowning in darkness as Conroy lays me on something flat, cold, hard. His hands stroke my cheeks.

"Get that mutt out of my tent!" An angry voice growls.

"Please, you've got to save him, Conroy begs. "He saved us. Please help him!" Sharp, shrill voices answer him.

Something cold is pulled over my nose. Fresh, clean air crosses my raw throat. I still can't see. Someone pries open my eyelids and drops something into my eyes. I clamp my eyelids tight. Someone forces open my jaw and sprays my throat. I cough and try to breathe. Darkness calls. I want the darkness. I want the burning to stop.

"What's that?" Conroy's voice asks.

"Salve for the eyes. Bicarbonate for the throat," explains a second voice, a kind voice, female. "It helps lessen the corrosion of the mucous membranes."

I don't know what that means, but it helps the burning. Breathing is easier, but it still burns.

"Now, move him off my gurney and out of my way." The harsh, barking voice is back.

Conroy picks me up and lays me on a pallet. He strokes my back.

"Father, help him. Let him live," Conroy prays. I fight the darkness. I hear Mama. *Be brave.* Conroy lies down on my pallet and drapes one arm around me. I feel safer with his arms there, and my insides start to calm. Gradually, his breathing slows, and I hear him slip to sleep. *I don't like this war, Mama.* I let the darkness come.

Later, as I struggle to awake, my mind floats back to the trench – the whine – the explosion – gasping for air. I twitch. I twitch and try to rouse myself, but I can't see. In the dark grey film of the room, someone murmurs, someone groans. Metal clinks against metal. Odors of pee and blood mingle with the smells of disinfectant. *The hospital.* I blink my eyelids again and again to clear the sticky film that covers them.

Gradually, I hear Conroy's voice creeping through the fog of my head. I smell his hand. He's still here.

"Stubby? Stubby?"

My tail thump, thump, thumps at the sound of his voice. I struggle to sit up. My eyes still burn as I force them open. Liquid drips down my cheeks. Through the haze, I make out a blurry face.

"Good Lord, Stubby! We thought you were dead!" Conroy takes a handful of fur on either side of my face. His forehead presses to mine, and he makes that silly noise like a human talking to her baby. But I don't care. He's here. My Conroy is here.

"Stubby!" His voice is excited now, and I feel his kiss on my head, my head that still throbs. I breathe in his scents and stick out my tongue to lick his face.

"You can take him." The female voice again. "He'll

be all right. Just let him rest a few days. That's the best thing for him."

"Now get that mutt out of here!" The other voice bellows from across the room.

"You betcha," says Conroy. Tenderly, he scoops me up in his arms and heads out. "Let's go home, partner."

For the next several days, Conroy leaves me at camp when he goes to work the trenches. I worry about him, but my orders are to stay and rest. I do, and I grow stronger.

At first, my nose is raw, and the scents are faint. Food loses all taste, and if I'm not watching, I can't tell who's coming and going. But the smells come back in a few days, and soon my nose is back on duty.

When Conroy comes in one evening, he's carrying a big black bundle.

"Look here," he says. He holds out the black thing toward my head. I see big eyes and a long nose. *A monster!*

Grr. My fur prickles.

"Come on, Stubby. It's okay," Conroy coaxes. "I made this for you. Look, it's like mine."

He picks up another black monster from his pack. "See, it's a mask. To keep out the gas."

Conroy pulls the black thing over his head. *Rrrr! Where's Conroy?* Then he takes it off, and there's Conroy.

"Come on, boy. Let's try this." I step back.

"Come on." I creep forward, eyeing the monster in his hands.

Standing stiff, I let him tie the thing on my head. It weighs heavy on my ears, but I can see through the eye holes. My breath is hot, the air stuffy.

"Hey, he's a real dogface now," Sam quips as he walks in.

Dogface? I feel more like a pig-face.

I exhale loudly, and my breath echoes in the mask. I sound menacing. I like that. *Now I'm the monster. Pig-face monster.* I breathe deep again and exhale even louder with an evil growl.

"You sound evil, partner." Conroy chuckles.

Conroy pulls my mask off and lays it aside. I welcome fresh air. I sniff at the mask and paw at it. I decide I like my own face best – and the fresh air.

I don't want to be a pig-face.

"Whose good mask did you cut up for that?" The voice snarls from the tent doorway. "Why are you wasting a soldier's mask on a dog?"

Billy! A growl builds up in the back of my throat.

Conroy ignores him.

"I said, whose mask is that!" Billy clenches a fist and starts toward Conroy.

"Hey, take it easy." Charlie jumps up between Conroy and Billy. Billy gives Charlie a shove, and Charlie trips over his own feet and sprawls back on the dirt.

Conroy pops up, heat flashing from his eyes.

"What do think you're . . ." Conroy ducks as Billy takes a swing. Billy misses. Conroy jabs him in the side.

My growl erupts. With a fierce bark, I start to leap in, but Charlie grabs my collar and holds me back. "Easy boy," he says. I bark a sharp warning at Billy, pulling tight against Charlie's hold, my ears laid back.

Billy swings with a wide right and misses Conroy again. Conroy grabs his arms and pins them behind him.

"What's wrong with you?" growls Conroy.

"Let go of me!" barks Billy. "You crazy . . ."

"Not till you settle down."

"What's going on here?" A sharp yell rips through the tent. Captain Raul enters.

"Uh, nothing, sir." Conroy drops Billy's arms and snaps to attention. He glares at Billy. "Just a misunderstanding." He's lying. I can smell it. *Why is he doing that?*

Billy, too, snaps to attention.

"That right?"

Billy's squinty eyes dart from Conroy to Charlie to me and then back to Conroy. "Yes, sir!"

The Captain glares at them for a long minute, silent.

"Well, let's have no more of it." The Captain turns and walks away, muttering to himself.

Billy harrumphs and stalks out of the tent.

With a deep exhale, Conroy plops down on his cot. "I don't get what his problem is."

I send a deep growl toward the empty doorway. *I could solve his problem. I'd love to shorten his nose for him.*

Charlie lets go of me, and I jump up next to Conroy. He scruffs my back. Another low growl escapes. Feeling my human's stress, I have to let it out a bit.

"Easy boy." Conroy keeps stroking. As he calms down, I do too.

Why can't humans be more like dogs? We don't fight unless there's a good reason — like food or females. We don't care what color you are or what your breed is. We don't hold a grudge. We just want to play — and eat — and get a good rub down or scratching.

I stare at the doorway.

Billy. I sense it's not over yet.

STUBBY'S WAR

13

"Is this where they keep the 'Yankees'?" A voice drawls from the doorway.

I spring up and pounce in front of the invader, growling, my ears flattened.

"Easy, boy. I'm on your side." A thin, sandy-haired soldier stoops and lowers his hand. I sniff his hand cautiously.

"This is 102nd, Yankee Division. Are you our new boys?"

"Yep. I'm Ellis. And this here's Frank."

"I'm Conroy. And that's my partner Stubby."

I venture a lick at Ellis's fingers. Salty. A trace of beef jerky.

"And I'm Sam. Where ya'll from?" Sam's voice drops into a drawl like theirs.

"I'm from Georgia, and Frank there's from

Mis'sippee." Frank takes off his cap and scratches his head. Although short on the sides, his black hair curls in loops on top – like a poodle's. He replaces his cap and flattens his curls.

"Virginia here," says Sam. "But Conroy's the real Yankee here – from Connecticut."

"Good to have you. Throw your stuff over there." Conroy motions toward some empty bunks.

Ellis and Frank fit right in, especially with Sam. They immediately liven up the place, laughing and telling jokes.

"C'mon, boys," says Sam. "Let's see what we're havin' for supper."

"Hope it's chicken." Frank pipes in. "By the way, Ellis, you think a three-week-old chicken's big enough to eat?"

"Naw, it'll be too small." Ellis blinks one eye. I wonder if he has something in it, but he grins.

"Then how's it gonna live if it can't eat?" Frank and Ellis cackle at their own joke; the other boys look blank.

"I doubt we've got any chicken," says Conroy. "Maybe some rubber bully beef if we're lucky."

We gather around the small fire a little later, me lying beside Conroy, one paw on his foot. Frank checks out his new rifle. He tries to insert one of the clips of what he calls a magazine, but he has it crooked or jammed or something. It won't go in. I still don't like guns. I don't know why the boys like them. But it's part of the job, so I stick close to Conroy.

"Dang, gun!" Frank slaps the barrel.

"Hold on, hold on." Conroy holds out his hand for the gun. "What's the problem? Didn't they teach you how to load these things?"

"These are sure different from our huntin' guns," mutters Frank.

"It's not that different," Conroy says. "Here, let me show you." He pops out the jammed clip and stands up. "Come over here. Let's work on it." With me by his side, he walks out of the light of the fire. Frank follows.

The sky above is clear, with a moon that doesn't hide the stars – millions of stars. But still, it is dark away from the fire. For the humans, that is. I can see fine.

"It's too dark to see what I'm doing," says Frank.

"Yeah, well, you've got to be able to do this by feel. Whether it's daylight or pitch black, without even looking down. You don't get to tell Ole Fritz you need some light so you can reload."

Frank follows Conroy's lead. Soon he loads and unloads the gun easily.

"You've got the hang of it," says Conroy. "Just keep practicing. And try to relax a bit.'

Conroy sits back down by the fire. I put my paws on his knees and lick his face, just to let him know that he's done a good job.

Morning comes too quickly.

Old scents greet us as we lead the new boys through the trench. Mud. Cigarettes. Mildew. Latrine. Rats. Familiar smells, but my gut knots up. With each step, my heart pounds faster.

My ears pull back and stick to my head. My legs feel heavy. I sniff. I listen for a whine . . . . I want to run!

Conroy stoops beside me.

"It's okay, buddy. You're thinking about that gas, aren't you, fella? It's okay. You've got a mask now. You'll be all right."

Conroy takes my face in his hands and tilts my face

toward his.

"It's okay," he repeats. "We're partners, remember? We look out for each other."

I give my lips a quick lick and try to relax my jaw. Conroy rubs me some more. His voice is calm. He smells calm.

Conroy stands. I give my body a vigorous shake and call up some courage.

Be brave.

We snake our way down the trenches, and the new boys eye the parapet.

"Can I look over?" asks Frank. I can smell his eagerness.

"Yeah but be careful. Old Fritz'll take a pot shot if he can."

Frank steps up the short ladder.

Zip! Bang! A shot scorches the dirt beside his head.

"Dang! I didn't even get my head up there."

We make our way a little farther down the trench.

"I'll try here," says Frank, and he steps on the rung of another ladder.

Zip! The shot bites the dirt and shoots grit into his eyes.

"Dang! How the hell does Fritz know what we're doin'?"

My nose twitches. My muscles tingle, my nose and ears itch, and even the hairs on my back. Something's not right. I trot on ahead to where the trench curves to the left. A few yards ahead, a soldier in an American uniform stands alone, watching our group. He's not one of my boys. A yellow bandana is tied to his bayonet. Something smells sour. I crouch to the ground, a low growl rumbling in my throat. My eyes flash to the steel barrel. I look back and forth between Frank and the soldier.

Frank steps back up on the first rung. The soldier down the trench raises his bandana.

Zip! Bang! The shot slices through the dirt. Frank falls back with a yowl!

"Gimme a rag!" Ellis yells and presses his hand against Frank's bleeding neck. Sam rushes to help him.

My growl bursts into a bark. I shoot over to the soldier with the bandana, with Conroy chasing after me. I'm airborne instantly and clamp my jaws on the arm holding the rifle.

"Stubby!" shouts Conroy, then he sees the bandana. "What the . . .. Hey! Smith! What do you think you're doing!" Conroy drops down on the soldier. He wrenches his rifle away and points it back at him.

Ellis flies across Conroy and tackles Smith to the ground, knocking me back into the mud. He starts to pound Smith with his fist.

"Back off, Ellis. I've got him." Conroy keeps the rifle pointed with one arm and pulls back Ellis with the other. "We'll let the Captain handle this. You take care of Frank."

My lips pull back, baring my fangs. Ready to attack.

"Easy, boy," says Conroy. "We've got him."

The soldier scowls at Conroy and clenches his jaw. He doesn't speak.

"Let's go," Conroy barks at Smith, disgust filling his voice.

Conroy pulls the soldier to his feet. "I said, let's go." His voice is growling. He looks back at Frank lying on the duckboards.

"You go ahead, Conroy. I'll help Ellis." Sam stoops down by Frank.

Sam and Ellis help Frank to the medic station. I keep up a warning growl as Conroy and I march our captive to the Captain. As I stand sentry, Conroy fills in the Captain on what happened.

"So, seems we've got ourselves a traitor, have we?" Captain Rous jerks the soldier around to face him. "You signaling old Fritz, boy?"

The prisoner gives the Captain a fierce stare but says nothing.

"I thought he was American," says Conroy. "Thought his name was Smith."

"I'm guessing that would be Schmidt," the Captain spews. "Well, we'll let the Colonel handle him back at base."

The Captain turns to Conroy. "So, ole Stubby caught himself a traitor, eh? Good job, Stubby."

I stand at attention at hearing my name. Only my tail rocks back and forth.

"I'll take it from here, Conroy. Get back to your men."

The rest of the morning drags on, with Sam and Ellis no longer in the mood for jokes or games.

Mid-afternoon, orders come down through the Captain.

"Let's get some rest, Stubby," Conroy says. "Looks like we're back on patrol tonight."

In the trenches, I continue learning all the habits and quirks and smells of the boys. I know Girard smells mischievous, Ellis smells loud, Sam smells like apples, Charlie smells kind, and Conroy smells calm and confident. I move freely among most of my boys, but there is one I stay away from -- Private Billy Moore. He smells mean-spirited. He constantly complains and says terrible things about the captains when they are out of earshot. One day when no one is looking, he kicks me in the ribs as hard as he can.

"You stupid mongrel!" he barks. "Why don't you go back where you came from?"

My ribs ache for hours. I stay out of his path.

I've learned Conroy's signals and remember to *come, stay, heel,* and, of course, *salute*. I also know *the signs for quiet, down, crawl,* and *forward*. Sometimes I can read Conroy's mind, and I start to obey before he even says the words. This makes him laugh, and he then gives me a good scratching – unless we're on patrol. Then it's all business until we get back. Even if I smell a rabbit, I stay on guard with my Conroy if we're on patrol. Work comes first – the backscratching comes later.

As we stand guard for hours in the trench, I make my rounds up and down the duckboards, keeping an eye on my boys. I smell the rats, but they'll keep for another time. I'm on patrol tonight. Under the dim moon and fog, we listen for the sounds of the night.

One evening as I'm making my rounds, the familiar scents of mud, latrine, and stale food flood my nostrils – then something else. I lap the air. The smell gets stronger – A biting bitterness burns my nose, my throat!

Gas! Burning Gas!

I dash around, barking wildly. Every hair stands on end. My insides quiver. *Woof!*

"What's up with him?" asks Sam.

"Stubby, hush!" orders Conroy. But I can't hush.

My legs shake, and my heart pounds. *It's coming!* I tilt my head back, snout toward the sky, and howl.

"Stubby, stop it! You're scaring the heck out of me!"

I clamp my jaw shut. I run around the legs of the boys. I *yap!* Run forward. Stop. *Woof!*

Then they, too, hear the faint whine getting louder and louder.

"Gas! Get your masks!"

"Stubby! Come here, Stubby!"

I run to Conroy. He straps on my pigface. Then he crouches down beside me and wraps his arm around my neck. The shells pop above us.

I exhale my hot breath through my monster mask. I breathe in. It's stuffy air but no gas. Conroy holds me tight. My gut still shivers. We huddle for a long while until the Captain signals that the danger is past.

"All clear," Conroy calls to the others. He unbuckles my mask, and I breathe in the welcome mud and rats and latrine– but only the faintest trace of gas. I give my body a vigorous shake from my nose to my tail.

"Next time, we'll listen to you, ol' boy!" Conroy says. Sam and Charlie take off their own masks and give me a good scratch on the back.

"Yeah, looks like we've got our own gas alarm," says Sam. "You just let us know when that's coming."

Woof! I survived!

Down the line, Billy pulls off his mask. He fixes his eyes on me in a hostile stare.

14

The rains return, and the cold seeps in. Still, we follow the Captain's instructions, ready our gear, and suit up for battle. Raindrops drip down my face. I blink them off. My boys stand in the rising flood— heads lowered as rain rolls off their helmets —ready and waiting for their signal.

Over time food has become scarce. Our regular rations of bully beef (canned corned beef) and stale biscuits are replaced with tough, stringy, dried beef. "Monkey meat," our French comrades call it.

"Not fit to eat!" Charles spits a wad in the dirt.

I take a bite. Don't see the problem. I've never seen a monkey, but this monkey meat is okay with me. *Just toss it over here, boys.*

It rains, and it rains, and it rains some more.

"It's raining cats and dogs," says Sam one evening.

Cats and dogs? I sit up and cock my head to the left, to the right. *No four-leggeds around except me.* Even the rats stay hidden in their dry burrows on nights like this. I curl back up next to Conroy and put my paw on his boot, just to let him know I'm here if he needs me.

At about midnight the mess boys come by with steaming hot coffee.

"That hits the spot," says Sam as he downs a cup.

"Yeah, kinda cuts through the cold," says Charlie. He takes his knife and scrapes mud from the side of his helmet.

At last, the rain draws to a drizzle, and the order comes down.

"Get ready. We go over the top tonight."

"We're gonna see real action this time." The raggedy old soldier plops down between Charlie and me. He launches a loogie, and it lands by my leg. I jump back. "Yep, regular out and out fighting. No more of this sitting around and waiting for them to blast us." His voice has me shaking again. I creep over and lie next to Conroy's foot. He rubs my back, and my insides calm down for a bit.

Conroy gives his rifle another check and then calls me to follow. He leads me down the trench and lets me sniff the soldiers going over. I memorize their scents as we pass. If someone falls in No Man's Land tonight, my nose will be able to find him. Most of my boys know me, but a few shift nervously as I approach them.

"Better not bite me," grumbles Captain Rous, but he still lets me sniff.

A few of the boys smirk when I nuzzle their crotches. A few wince, but most are grateful. I walk through the line and memorize their individual scents mixed with two scents shared by all – determination and fear.

Only Billy shoves me away, mumbling and swearing under his breath.

Then we wait, quiet, each man lost in his own thoughts.

My paw itches, and I bite at it, again and again, until it hurts – just a little.

Be brave. A voice whispers in my head.

I nuzzle Conroy's leg, and he scratches my ear. My muscles ripple with anticipation. Sam taps his rifle stock nervously. Ellis bows his head in prayer.

"Fix bayonets!" Captain Rous's sudden order echoes down the lines.

Metal clinks on metal as the boys attach the deadly points on their rifles.

Boom!

Our first rockets shoot up from the trenches and soar toward the enemy trenches from behind us.

"Softening 'em up for us." Sam's tap, tap, tap of his fingers on the rifle barrel grows more rapid.

"Yeah, Big Bertha! Pound 'em for us. Pound 'em into marmalade!" Ellis's smile is grim. The trench reeks of nervousness and, for the first time – fear.

The ground rumbles as more rockets arc overhead and light up the sky, raining down bright greens and yellows.

"Over the top!"

The boys scramble over the parapet. I start to follow.

"Stubby, you stay here!" Conroy shouts. I bark to object, but he finds a foothold, pulls himself over the top and is gone.

Stay here? No way! My insides jiggle. *I want to go!* I sprint back and forth up the abandoned trench until I spot some supply boxes and climb up and over.

I bound after them, both hind legs pumping.

Mud erupts in little spats as bullets bite the ground and mingle with the dark. Tracking the sounds of our soldiers, I rush across the field and close in on my boys.

"Down!" The Captain shouts. My body flattens as enemy bullets overshoot our lines.

Up again, I rush on, then slip, slide, and tumble down into a muddy shell crater. I fall over a warm body and suck in his scent. *Ellis!* But mixed in with his smell is the warm, metallic scent of blood. A dark stain spreads across his sleeve.

"Hey, buddy." Ellis coughs mud from his throat. "They got my good arm, fella. But you tell the others I'm okay."

I answer Ellis with a low whimper and a lick across his face; then, I scramble out to find Conroy.

As I make a mad canter up and down the line, rifle butts clash, and bayonets clang. The fight is man against man, bayonet against bayonet. Mud coats the uniforms and makes it hard to tell friend from foe, but my nose can tell.

Everywhere is chaos. Barbed wire tangles are torn from their posts and strung across the field. As the fight wears on, weapons and supplies and fallen soldiers lie abandoned on the field.

Finally, the wall of German troops begins to break apart into groups. Still, behind the front line, another swarm approaches with bayonets drawn, like ants on a kicked-up ant hill.

Where's Conroy?

I see movement on my left and spot Ellis dragging himself over a pile of sandbags camouflaging a machine gun stand. His face contorts with pain. I run over. Beside him, splayed face down in the mud, lies a German soldier.

Ellis presses his chest against the gun and turns it toward the approaching swarm of the enemy. With a grunt, he reaches for the trigger.

Rat – a tat – tat – tat –tat! The gun rattles his arm and roars as it spits fire. The enemy line flattens like grass blades under a boot.

Rat –a tat – tat – tat! Our gun is echoed by another one confiscated across the field.

"Woo – hoo!" yells Ellis. His eyes flash with energy. "That's the way to do it!"

"Woo – hoo!" I bark back. Caught up in the yelling and running and booming and spraying dirt, I can't feel my insides shake. I feel like a canine warrior. I want to *howl!* louder than the bombs and the guns. *"Woo – hoo!"*

I peek over the sandbags and watch as the Germans pull back. Our boys swoop around them.

"*Kamerad*! Surrender!" At last, the Germans in the front line call out when they see they're surrounded. In a daze, they permit our boys to round them up and march them back toward camp.

As they pass us, Ellis and I fall in beside the captives. Ellis uses his good arm to clench his wounded one tightly to his chest. His face winces, but his eyes gleam.

We cross back over the German's first trench, now mostly filled with dirt and rocks and sandbags from the shelling. Ellis trips over a strand of loose barbed wire.

The enemy captain behind him sees his chance. Quickly and silently, he retrieves a trench knife from his boot, grabs Ellis in a chokehold, and sticks the knife to his neck. Ellis's cry is choked silent. But not mine.

Like lightning, I growl and lunge for the hand holding the knife. I clampdown.

With a howl of rage and pain, the soldier drops the knife and swings his arm to throw me off. I hold on. A nearby Doughboy, called Owens, hears the yell -- and, in a flash, knocks the enemy to the ground and pins his arms.

The enemy sputters out curses in German, but the boys and I understand. Anger is universal.

"Looks like somebody's mad as a hornet." Owens

spits mud as he ties the man's wrists and marches him forward.

"Yep. Wouldn't want to be bit by him now. He's as mad as a rabid dog!" says Ellis. He huffs and clutches his bad arm to his side.

I bark an instant objection. *What did he mean - rabid dog?*

"Oh no, boy!" says Ellis as he squats beside me, and I lick his face. "I'm not talking about you, fella. Looks like you saved me again."

"*Woof!*" I answer. *That's more like it.*

But what I really want is Conroy. *Where is he?*

Lines of the soldiers drag back to our trenches. I sniff and search their weary faces as they pick their steps through the blanket of dead soldiers. At last, I hear his voice.

Conroy! I spot him trudging up ahead. The energy of the battle shoots through me again.

"*Woohoo!*" I bark as I bound over to him.

But my energy drains when I see the fatigue on my partner's face.

"Hey, boy." He stoops and holds my face. Exhaustion fills his eyes. "It's over for tonight, partner. Let's go home."

Conroy stands and wipes the grime and sweat from his face. In silence, we march back toward the trench.

15

Between midnight and dawn, a star shell rises and bursts overhead, casting a greenish light over the trenches and the craters of No Man's Land.

"Fritz ain't asleep," Sam grumbles as he shakes off his sleep.

"Sounds like they're regrouping," says Captain Rous. "Let's see if we can find any of our boys while it's still quiet out there."

"Come on, Stubby." Conroy pulls on his black coveralls. "Let's suit up."

It's over the top again. And again, I lead my boys through the wasteland scarred by muddy craters from bombs and artillery shells. Naked trees stretch out menacing arms like monsters, with bodies of dead and injured men swallowed in their shadows.

We moved stealthily, listening for breathing in the dark. This is my specialty. My ears pick up the sound, and the scent, of our wounded Doughboys, and I lead Conroy and his patrol to them.

"Uhhh..." A low groan drifts in the wind. I stop and twitch one ear. As I turn in the direction of the voice, I stick my nose in the air and sniff. *French.* With only the faintest yip, I tug on Conroy's pant leg in the direction of the groan. He knows to follow, and I silently lead him to our wounded comrade. Conroy and his crew pull him back to safety, and we move on to find the next one. Even when a soldier can't call out, my nose can find him.

The Captain has begun to depend on me in this reconnaissance. My work is important, and Conroy is proud of me. That makes me happy.

But these nightly missions remain perilous, and I am ever watchful for the German soldiers collecting their own injured.

Both teams of night warriors, clad in black, move, furtive as mice, over the shell-pocked wasteland, looking for the wounded and staying far afield from the other team if possible. We inch noiselessly, stopping and listening for the crunch of enemy boots, dropping flat in a death-like pose when a German star shell sends its greenish light arcing above. We slither through the mud on our bellies.

Quiet as cats, we creep back, and Conroy gives me a good rub down and tells me I've done a good job. As my head rests on his lap, curls of satisfaction wiggle through me.

The next night begins much like the others. I lead my boys through the drizzle in search of our wounded and scout for the enemy. We crouch along, single file, dodging shell holes. About midway across, I freeze and lift my nose.

To the right, I spot a German patrol heading in our opposite direction. Roughly the same number of boys as us. Conroy follows my gaze. He spots the German soldiers at the same time that they spot us. A low growl gurgles in my throat.

"Shhh," Conroy whispers. The Germans halt. Both sides remain motionless, studying each other for a long minute. Charlie raises his rifle, but Conroy places his hand on it. Charlie lowers it again. I smell the tension. I will my insides not to shake. My paw itches, but I keep my eye on the Germans. We wait, both sides still and silent. At last, the Germans slowly walk off in the direction they are heading. No shots fired; no bombs thrown.

"Well, I'll be," whispers Charlie.

The rest of the patrol goes without incident. The boys are quiet until they rest back at the camp.

"What do you think?" asks Charlie.

Conroy puts aside his helmet and checks his rifle.

"I think those boys wanted to get back home tonight just as much as we did," Conroy offers in a low voice. "We could have shot them, I suppose. Maybe we should have. They could have shot us. Probably will tomorrow. But tonight – well, we've all got a chance to be here for tomorrow."

Conroy readies his gear and lies down. Under his bunk, I lick my paw until I hear his breathing grow slow and steady. The German boys – are they in their bunks?

Will we see those boys tomorrow?

STUBBY'S WAR

16

Rain pelts my skin with cold, hard drops as we march – or slog – down the muddy, shell-pocked road.

We march behind a long line of horses bearing French officers and pulling a wagon with a giant gun that Conroy calls a howitzer. We wind like a long caterpillar through the narrow roads. When we first trained with the Frenchmen, I tried to stop and sniff each time a horse dumped his droppings in front of me. Conroy's nudges and harsh words stopped that, so now I just sneak a whiff as I trot around the piles.

On we march through the drizzling rain, for five days, Conroy says. I plod alongside Conroy, the mud sucking at my paws. We see rolling fields from the road, dotted occasionally by white smoke curling up from tall chimneys beside the small farmhouses. I catch the scents of horses and chickens, raccoons and rabbits, and mice. Another scent comes – coyote, sharp and musty, mixed with fur, saliva, mud, and grass. I can tell the coyote is far off, deep in the woods. A wild deer stands motionless at the edge of the woods, staring wide-eyed. I itch for a chase, but I'm working now, so I stick with Conroy.

Occasionally we meet war-worn French troops heading back from the front. Sometimes white ambulance trucks roll by, with big red crosses painted on the side panels. Our wounded are heading home.

We meet two kinds of soldiers. Young, cheery boys are marching toward their first battle, bragging and laughing and whistling, as my boys did in the beginning. But sadder men marching back, haggard and wounded, with weary eyes.

We meet companies herding slump-shouldered German prisoners-of-war, hands tied behind their backs. I stare at the enemy, wanting to growl. But these are not strong soldiers like the ones we captured before. Many of these prisoners are bony and gray-haired or young and baby-faced, looking barely big enough to carry a rifle. I remember the first Fritz my boys caught. Just a boy.

"Grandpas and kids!" Ellis calls out as we move over to let a group pass. "Ol' Fritz is robbing the cradle and the grave." He points with his arm still wrapped in a bandage.

"Must be running out of able-bodied soldiers," says Sam.

"Not all of them," says Conroy. "Look at that big brute there. He's as big as an ox!"

He motions to a massive German waving his arms wildly and spitting at his captors. Even under guard, he smells savage.

"He does seem a little peeved."

"I think he's frothing at the mouth," Ellis joins in, "like a mad dog."

Mad dog! Where? I back up and growl.

"Don't worry, Stubby." Conroy laughs and whistles me back.

I growl at the ox. Meanness radiates from him.

"That's it, Stubby," says Ellis. "You tell him to play nice, now."

"Just keep your eye on him," says Conroy. "He's bad medicine."

At Conroy's side, I give a low growl and keep on guard.

"The rest of them are probably glad to be out of those trenches," says Sam. "At least our side will keep them safe and feed them."

"Yeah, well, they'll have to trade their kraut for some peas." Ellis digs a piece of jerky from his pocket and tears off a bite. I trot over and look up for a taste. "Speaking of which, I could sure use some peas and cornbread right now."

"I don't think the French know how to make cornbread," says Sam. "Least I haven't seen any."

"Sure would like some, though." Ellis tosses a bite of jerky. I catch it midair. "Maybe some corn and beef tips, too."

Beef? I bark my agreement.

We pack into a motor truck and lumber down a wider road on the fifth day. Stuck on the floorboard among the soldiers' legs, I smell sweat and damp feet and fungus mixed in with cigarettes, gasoline, and grease.

I cough.

"Stuffy down there?" Conroy pulls me up in his lap. I stick my nose to the crack between the sideboards and suck in the fresh air. Still rainy; still cold. But I smell a faint hint of Spring trying to creep out of the muddy ground. The truck motor grinds and grunts as the driver gears down to climb the hills or straddle the ruts in the road.

Hours later, the motor truck rumbles to a stop. I jump off and rush to the nearest bush and hike my leg. You can put off some things just so long.

Happy to be on solid ground, I scamper around and sniff for a rabbit. Before I take off after my furry prey, I glance back at my boys. Good thing, too – they're throwing their gear aboard and climbing up in a freight train idling on the tracks.

Forgetting the rabbit, I shoot back beside Conroy – just in time for him to hoist me up into the train car. Nestled at Conroy's feet, I relax as his fingers move back and forth across my back.

"Good boy," he coos. "Good boy." When he tries to stop rubbing, I paw him for more. I like the smell of his sweat and the firm rub of his hands across my back. The clang of the metal rails and methodical puffing of the steam engine soon lull me asleep.

"Seicheprey!" calls the Captain. "Everybody off." His voice chases the rabbits out of my dreams.

17

My boys and I are allowed a couple of days' rest as we billet in the village. They are given much-needed fresh clothes and equipment, including the desperately needed new boots.

"Hallelujah!" The boys shout as they shed their wet, ragged boots and pull on the new ones. I nibble at my paw pads and pull out a stem and a rock from between my toes. I'm ready to go.

Spring is squeezing through the mud, and the rabbits are multiplying. No need to eat them since I'm fed every day. But I taunt them for hours. I spot their noses twitching in the underbrush as they scout for tender new shoots of green. I lurk in shadows until they hop farther away from the briars.

Then I pounce! I circle and leap and growl until I see them shiver and cower. Pretending to lose interest, I back away, giving them space to escape. Then I bark and pounce once more and chase them back into the briars. *I am Lord of the Chase!*

But more fun than rabbits are the children.

The children smell good – like cheese, grape juice, and dirt. They play outside every day, but not far from home. I make instant friends. They seem amazed at how adept I am at a game of fetch. I mean, how hard is it? You toss a stick. I retrieve it. Not hard to do. But the children are amused, and I like the attention. When they are called in by their parents, I go exploring.

Seicheprey is a tiny village nestled among rolling hills and heavy woods. For weeks, it has been at the edge of the fighting. Conroy says it hasn't been under direct attack, but random shells have flattened buildings and sometimes whole blocks.

Conroy points out signs that dot the storefronts: "Safe cellar here." When the shells rain down, spattering mud and dirt upon passing villagers, they dart for the nearest shelter to wait out the storm. Then they come out and go about their business.

"It's sad that it's become normal for them," says Sam. "That war is normal."

When Conroy and Sam stop to help an older lady take in some firewood, I wander down a side street. Two gray-haired ladies in dark dresses and cotton stockings sit outside a small cottage. In front of them, propped on old chair backs, rests a wood frame. The women's fingers push needles up and down through patchwork fabric stretched on the racks. They chitter softly with each other. Dropping her head back suddenly, one chuckles aloud. She tightens the scarf under her chin and cuts her eyes at her friend, whose shoulders shake as she joins in the secret laugh.

I venture closer, sniffing. Potatoes, lard, flour . . .

Maybe a cake in her pocket? I nuzzle my nose, sniffing her hand.

"*Ouste!*" Smack! My nose stings, and I back off.

The ladies chuckle again and resume the up and down, in and out, of the needles.

Down the street, off-duty Doughboys play catch with the children or mend their toys or give out any sweets they can find in their pockets. A few of them play with the babies, draw water, or carry firewood or peel potatoes, helping with anything they find a French woman doing.

Another street looks abandoned – with windows blown out, no women, no children. Amid the rubble stands the ruined shell of a church – stained glass shattered, roofs gone, walls burned and crumbling, even the bronze bells melted into a heap. The entire block seems flattened except for one tall statue standing in the middle of the destruction. I dig around the base, kicking up scraps of wood, cloth, and broken glass. Roaches and beetles scurry when I kick off their shelter.

In the middle of the square and on top of a pillar stands the figure of a girl, her legs clad in high-top boots. She looks like she's marching, her eyes raised to the sky. She holds her chin up, defiant and daring. Around her waist is tied a scabbard and a sword. In her left hand, she raises a broken flagstaff, the top and bottom parts blown off by shells. Her right arm points forward, her index finger-pointing, the tip missing.

I go back to digging. I scratch around for a lizard. Nothing.

"*Saint Jeanne d'Arc.*" The French voice startles me.

A young girl, around 10, sits down on the rubble and holds out her hand. My nostrils twitch, smelling berries on her fingers.

"*Saint Jeanne d'Arc.*" She repeats in French.

I give myself a shake, and my dog tags clink. When I cock my head, she wiggles her fingers. Moving in close, I nuzzle her arm. *Maybe she'll share the berries.* She leans forward and scratches my head.

"Some people thought she was a witch, you know."

I blink and lick her fingers. I look for a pocket. She keeps scratching my neck and talking. The scratching feels good. *A treat would be better.*

"But she wasn't. Jeanne d'Arc was a real hero. She led the French army to victory at Orleans."

I lick her face. She definitely had berries. I turn and let her scratch my other side.

"She's not really a saint yet, but *Mémé* says she ought to be. But she was a hero, and I'm going to be a hero just like her when I grow up."

Hero? A short whine escapes as I think of Mama, but I shake it off.

"Jeanne! There you are. I've been looking for you." A young boy pants as he calls up the street. "*Maman* says to come in. You're not supposed to be down here."

I cock my head, and the girl laughs.

"*Oui*, that's right. My name's Jeanne, too. *Mémé* says I'm named after her."

"Coming, Jean-Paul. Wait up for me!" Jeanne digs into her pocket. I sit up, ready for a berry. But all she has is a small metal disc. A bit of cracker hits the ground, though, and I snap it up before she can get it.

"Here. Pépé brought this back from Domrémy, Where Jeanne d'Arc was born. It's just a souvenir, but now you have a medal." She pins the disc to my collar and starts off after her brother.

I start to follow but stop and look back at the statue. The medal clinks against my dog tags.

A hero.

A shell explodes up the street, and I flatten instantly. When the dirt stops raining, Jeanne is gone.

STUBBY'S WAR

18

The night guards spy German patrols from our trench outside the village, but we wait for orders to engage. Rumors ripple back that the Fritz is planning a major onslaught on our tiny town, so my boys prepare. These trenches remain from the last battle here, but we resupply them and ready our weapons.

Then we wait. But not for long.

A cold, light rain falls around midnight, morphing into a dense fog as morning nears. I sleep in snatches amid all the shuffling along the duckboards.

Boom! Boom!

Sudden shells strike like a volley of thunderbolts.

"It's 3:00 a.m.," mutters Sam. "Don't they sleep?" He pulls his blanket tighter around his shoulders and leans against the dirt wall.

For about an hour, we are blasted by high explosives. I huddle next to Conroy. Then I hear a dreaded whine and get the first sniff of the death cloud.

I bark loud and sharp. *Gas!* I yelp! *Gas!* I bury my nose under Conroy's arm. The Captain knows my warning.

"Gas! Incoming!" We hear the canister scrape across the rocks as the boys grab their masks and hunker down. Conroy holds my mask tight on my face for long, long minutes, but I can't stop the trembling. At last, the Captain signals all clear.

Whiz, bang! Boom! Rat-a-tat-tat-tat! Shots ring out. The artillery bombardment resumes, relentless. Large sections of our trenches are leveled. Soldiers dig out comrades buried by collapsing walls.

At last, the shelling quiets. I pick my way down the trench to check on my boys. Though covered in dirt, they have survived, too.

Corporal Blanchard sits on the duckboards, staring at his leg. A three-inch piece of shrapnel protrudes from his calf.

"Make a pretty good souvenir, don't you think?" He grimaces and yanks the shard from his leg. He ties a handkerchief around the wound to stop the bleeding. I sneeze at the scent of fresh blood.

"It'll take more than that to stop us." Blanchard grabs the wall. Conroy offers a hand, and he struggles to his feet.

Conroy pats my shoulder. "Time to get ready, Stubby." He points down the line of boys. "Go!"

Once again, I trot down the line and sniff my boys, especially any newcomers. Billy snorts a warning, and I skirt around him. Afterward, I sit tight next to Conroy, feeling like a sitting duck as we wait for orders to strike. My paw itches. I try to ignore it. The minutes wear on, and I feel Conroy's muscles grow tighter.

"Fix bayonet!" The Captain barks the command.

Anxiousness surges through the trench. Cold nerve coats the faces of my boys. My back quivers. *Be brave.* I look up at Conroy. *I'm ready.*

In the early gray dawn, the air rumbles. German shock troops charge across Dead Man's Land with a torrent of fire. As they cross the halfway mark, the command echoes down the line:

"Over the top!"

Our counter-barrage begins.

Boom!

Shells from our own tanks behind us arc overhead and explode the German trenches. I weave among my boys as we plow forward.

The first part of our charge is easy. I dart around the shell craters, kicking dirt in my wake. A few of my boys slip and tumble into the muddy holes, but they clamber out and keep going. Like hunting dogs off the leash, we race on, wind whipping our faces.

Many Germans drop under our barrage of shells, but great waves come on. Our guns bark fire, but the enemy guns bark back.

"Down, men, down!" yells the Captain, and we flatten ourselves in the mud.

"Up! Men, up!" We scramble up and surge forward.

Bullets rain around us, tearing gaps in our line of soldiers. Still, my boys press on. A shell blasts the earth near Sam. He dives for the dirt and rolls over, covering his head. Seconds later, again on his feet, he charges forward. I dart among my boys, barking encouragement. My brave boys, charging like fierce hunters.

We reach the tangled wire in front of the enemy trenches, and the Germans climb out to meet us head-on. And we fight – hand-to-hand, bayonet-on-bayonet – the battle of the wild – kill or be killed.

Dirt kicks up in my face, stinging my eyes. I dart back and forth in the middle of the fray, watching my boys and nipping the ankles of the enemy. I find Conroy in a bayonet duel with a massive German. Clanks and jabs and thrusts sway back and forth. The enormous German looms over Conroy like a bull over a hound, but the hound is quick and furious. I dash around, trying to snap at the German. Then with a fierce lunge, Conroy's bayonet finds its mark.

The massive German grunts, staggers, and falls flat back -- trapping my hind legs under his body. I *yelp*! and dig like a drowning cat with my front legs. Conroy's head jerks toward me; then, in one sweeping motion, he grabs my collar, yanks me loose, and charges on toward the next German. I shake out my legs. Unhurt, I bound after him.

Our boys fight fiercely from ambush and in the open. Germans blast us with bullets and even liquid fire from flamethrowers. We answer with grenades, rifles, and machine guns.

Back and forth, the battle sways, each side fighting furiously. The clang of metal on metal, the thump of bodies hitting the mud, the yells, the smoke, the smell of gunpowder and blood. In the chaos, I tear around, checking for my boys.

The battle spreads from the trenches to the streets of the town. Villagers slam and bolt their doors.

In and out of the streets of Seicheprey, in the little public square, and in the small cottage yards, we fight.

Down the lines echo the chants: "Hold 'em! Hold 'em!"

But, outnumbering our boys eight to one, waves of Germans keep rolling in. By noon they're commanding most of the shell-stripped streets. Our boys pull back to regroup for the counterattack.

Sam and Charlie plop down next to a skeleton tree,

panting and flushed, pulling out canteens to wash dirt and smoke from their throats. With a "Woohoo!" from Ellis, he and Conroy slide onto the ground beside them. I lap water from Conroy's sweaty hand. He rubs my neck, and my heart's rapid thump, thump, thump begins to steady. But we stay on alert.

Night falls again, and we set out for our counterattack. My boys creep forward with white-heat determination.

"If Ol' Fritz thinks we're gonna lie down and give up, he's got another thing comin'," whispers Ellis as we crawl through the darkness.

"Shhhh! Don't you have any sense? There's patrols out here," Billy hisses.

"I said no smoking, no lights, no talking!" growls the Captain.

My eyes, nose, and ears keep alert for the enemy as we advance through the dark. We move along a well-camouflaged and torn-up road until we come to a garden gate that is still standing. Then we creep close together in the blackness. As we cross rock formations, we risk being spotted. The enemy sends up flares, and we freeze in position, like trees or posts, and then creep on.

The Captain motions for a halt and orders a machine gunner at each end of our group. A bayonet man keeps guard on either side. In silence, the rest of us sit down to wait.

Conroy holds my face tight against his cheek as we listen.

"Now!" commands the Captain. We leap up and charge the enemy.

The enemy, surprised but recovering, fires back with

machine guns and grenades. Our first man falls. I scoot over. A Frenchman. Almost completely covered with dirt, the blood pumps from his mouth, his ears, and his eyes. He chokes and lies still. The life scent evaporates, replaced with that of death. I rush after Conroy.

The battle lasts until the first fingers of dawn, and still, the Germans come on, jumping over their dead and fallen comrades, only to be mowed down by our guns. Shouts and screams of the wounded and dying squeal in my ears, along with the *rat-a-tat-tat-tat* of machine-gun fire and the clangs of bayonets and rifles.

At last, the Germans pull back behind their trenches. The stragglers and the wounded surrender under waves of lifted arms.

"*Kamerad!*" they call, as they lift up their hands. My boys round them up and disarm them. I circle around our captives and nip at their heels to keep them in line.

We discover several days' rations and extra trench tools as we collect their weapons and haversacks. Some boys pocket the extra grub for later.

"Looks like they were ready for the long haul." Sam tears a chunk of bread and tosses it to me. I gulp it greedily.

"Yeah, but they underestimated our boys," Ellis answers, as he stuffs some bread in his pocket. I sniff and nudge his arm. He relents and shares a little with me.

Some of our boys march the captives back to our command post. Conroy and I wait in the trench and watch for any further attack.

"*Grrrr.*" I low-growl a warning. My ears rotate in the direction of the sound. Boot steps.

"Hush." Conroy, too, hears the steps and readies his bayonet.

The noise stops, and we freeze, quiet as rocks. A

head rises over the parapet, and Conroy draws back, ready to lunge his bayonet . . . .

"Help me!" A desperate cry is choked out. The white, contorted face of one of our French comrades peers over. His eyes roll back, and he collapses. Conroy and Charlie grab his arms and pull him into the trench. Several red splotches seep across his coat, but he's still breathing. He opens his eyes, and Conroy pours water into his mouth. Charlie runs back for the medics, who come with a stretcher and load up the injured man. The ground where they drag him is stained with fresh blood.

The battle lulls, but not for long. Soon, we hear the familiar whine and boom of rocket shells overhead.

"Looks like we've got a party coming." Charlie readies his weapons.

Along the trench, soldiers clink their bayonets to their rifles.

"Just star shells," says Ellis.

"Why haven't we heard the ground guns coming?" Charlie shifts his weight, ready to go.

"Just wait," Conroy cautions. He leans back against the mud wall.

All is silent. I fidget and sniff the air for a clue. I need to see. I scoot over and scramble up the boxes to the top of the parapet.

"No, Stubby! Down. Now!" Conroy yells and lunges to grab me. But too late.

I hear a long, high-pitched whine, then . . .

Boom!

The night lights up as the ground explodes with flying rock and mud and barbed wire.

I am blown back onto the duckboards. Fire knifes through me.

Sliding my head in the dirt, I look down at my body. Shards of metal protrude from my flank and foreleg.

I can't get up.

The ground spins.

Pain draws a jagged line up to my head. The world grows blurry.

"Stuuuubyyyy!"

Conroy's cries echo and grow fainter as I fall into a deep black hole.

PART THREE - Wounded Warriors

19

The clink of glass and rhythmic *woosh, woosh* of labored breathing pulls me back to consciousness. *Where am I?* I sneeze. I recognize the antiseptic smell.

Faint voices grow louder. I yip softly, *Conroy! Where are you?*

"Hey, fellow. It's about time you woke up." My tail wags at his voice.

I struggle, but I can't get up. I lie on my side; my legs and shoulders are strapped down. My flank feels numb. I crane my nose down so I can see. Conroy lies in the next bunk, a white bandage wrapped around his head, across one eye.

"You really gave us a scare, old boy."

"You both gave us a scare, Conroy." I stretch my head upward, recognizing the new voice, Sam. "How ya' doin'? How's Stubby?"

"Hey, Sam! Good of you to come. Doc says Stubby'll

be all right." Conroy sits up and hangs his legs off the bunk.

"Thanks to you." Sam reaches out and pats my side. "I never saw anybody run so fast as you did with that dog. And half-blind, too, after that shrapnel swiped your head and eye."

"Just taking care of my partner. Doc says I'll be out of here by tomorrow, but they're keeping Stubby for a few more days. That shrapnel went deep."

Partner, I hear through the fog. My heart thumps in my chest.

"Don't worry about Stubby," says Sam. "He'll be having the nurses and the patients hand-feeding him bacon before the week's over."

Drool collects at the thought of bacon. But all I smell is mud and alcohol and blood. Am I awake? I really want to sit up. I whimper. Foggy images swirl in my head, my Mama's face fading in the distance. Pain rips through my side.

"Easy partner," soothes Conroy. He strokes my chin and whispers, "You're a good boy. You'll be all right."

I lick his fingers and savor his familiar, salty taste. I inhale his scent, and my pounding pulse relaxes.

Partner, he said. I'm his partner.

The blanket pallet is cold on the floor when I wake up. One of my legs is wrapped in white gauze, but I can stand on the other three. The room spins around. I shake my head. I feel woozy and topple back down.

Antiseptic smells swirl around the medic tent, mixed with urine, blood, and gunpowder. My ears ring with the clanging of metal pans. Muffled voices. Shuffling feet. I push up to a three-legged stand. The room swims. I shake my head. Dizziness settles a bit. I lap some water from a nearby bowl. I want to leave. I step and stumble but stay standing. I need to go.

But go where? Conroy is gone.

Lifting my head, I draw in a long breath through my nose but find no scent of Conroy. I hobble around the room, trying to pick up his smell. Then I head toward the door at the end.

"Don't worry, Stubby. He'll be back." An assuring voice comes from a soldier in a nearby cot. "Conroy's told me all about you. I told him I'd look after you."

The soldier's eyes are warm. I hobble over to him. He has one arm bandaged and strapped to his chest. One leg is wrapped and ends in a stub where his foot should be. I look back at his face.

"Yep," he says. "I guess now I'm a Stubby, too." He forces a chuckle, but I see the pain in his eyes. He drops his good hand off the cot. I lick it and nose his arm.

"How's Barney Baby doing today?" A pretty, young lady carries fresh bandages to the soldier's cot and begins redressing his wounds. Her dark sleeves are rolled up above the elbows. Over the front of her dress is tied a white apron. A matching white scarf binds back her curly dark hair.

"You keep calling me 'baby,' and I'll get better every day, Nurse Ellen," answers Barney, bobbing his eyebrows in a tease. I back under his cot and out of the way.

"That's Nurse Borg to you, soldier," she chides, but her lips crinkle in a smile.

I look at the soldiers lying on the cots and filing into my tented room. I have fared better than many of my comrades.

Ambulances roll in, and new wounded soldiers arrive, borne on stretchers or wearily stumbling, wrapped in blankets or coats, bandaged or splinted. All are stiff with mud or caked with blood. Pale and cold, many of them cannot speak but merely point to their attached labels describing their injuries.

From my pallet, I study them all – looking and sniffing. *Lots of soldiers. But no Conroy.*

Over the grassy floor, medics push in a line of stretchers of wounded soldiers -- some with hanging or missing limbs, some with heads wrapped in bloody bandages, some missing parts of their faces – all the handiwork of rifle bullets or bayonets or shrapnel like what hit me. A few of them limp in with the aid of other soldiers or medics.

"John and me got buried alive!" says one soldier, who says his name is Edward. "Old Boche shelled our trench, and it caved in on us. Thank goodness those Frenchmen dug us out." Only his eyes and mouth shine through the mud over his head and body. He spits continually and holds his left arm -- bent at a strange angle above the wrist – close to his chest with his right hand. His voice lowers. "Claude and Peter didn't make it."

More soldiers come in unconscious or gasping for breath, clutching broken ribs, coughing, and spitting dirt and blood. Some stink of rotting meat. "Gangrene," I hear a nurse say as she meets the eyes of a medic.

The moans are desperate.

"Morphine!" Some call out to the nurses. "Please, help me!"

Other soldiers emit a low, whining, constant groan. A few soldiers jerk and talk to themselves. I remember my own twitches from bad dreams and wonder what horror these soldiers are reliving.

The nurses work among them methodically, reading charts, uttering low encouragements, and administering morphine.

Be brave, my Mama said. These soldiers were brave, and I can be brave, too.

Sharp pains rip my side with my first steps after my injury, but gradually I heal. Every day I make my rounds among the wounded, always watching for Conroy.

A line of soldiers files in one day, all with faces bandaged, some bleeding through. They stumble in, silent, each with his hands on the shoulders of the soldier in front of him, the first being led by a rumpled, raisin-faced old man, the only one who can see. He leads them in, and they slump down along a wall and wait for the medic. I hobble over and nuzzle encouragement. Some of them ignore me; a couple of them start to cry, their tears invisible under the bandage. I know they need me, so I keep nosing their arms or licking their hands.

The saddest of the wounded, though, are the burn victims. "Flamethrowers," the medics say. Fritz has armed his soldiers with flame throwers in recent battles, and the victims suffer melted flesh from the liquid fire. The stench of burnt flesh emanates from their limbs.

"How can any man do this to another," cries a new young nurse when she sees her first victim.

The burn victims often have their whole faces wrapped, as well as their arms and torsos.

Those are the ones I go to first. I paw at their covers and whimper to let them know I am there. Sometimes they move an arm, and I nudge it back, sniffing the salve and ruined flesh. Often, I'm answered with only silence. I listen for their faint breathing, sensing it will be a miracle if they survive.

As the wounded come in, the intake nurses divide them into those stretcher-bound on one side and those able to stand on the other. And then the worst cases are sent to "resuss" or "pre-op." The lighter cases are sent to "evac" for stitches and splints and a return to combat.

Some men lie uncomplaining despite shattered heads, disfigured faces, or missing limbs. Some are spitting blood or struggling to breathe. A few are afraid to be touched, but I know they still need me.

I nudge a hand dangling from a bed with my nose; I offer a soothing whimper. The soldier almost always returns with a scratch on my nose, often with a pained smile.

When the intake room becomes too chaotic for me to help, I visit the pre-op or evacuation rooms, where soldiers are able to scratch my head and tell me about their own dogs back home.

Then I retire to my pallet and rest for the next day.

"Incoming!" A medic bursts through the door, pushing a stretcher.

Suddenly awake, I scoot under Barney's cot.

On the stretcher lies a thin, gaunt-looking soldier, looking much older than most of the young boys. A shock of iron-gray hair, stiff with blood and dirt, sticks out above a forehead pinched in pain.

Old Jeb! Old Jeb's hurt? I scoot out from under the cot to get a closer look.

"Out of my way, dog!" The husky medic shoos me back with his foot.

The old soldier gurgles as he pants for breath. The

medics lay open his uniform.

Blue . . . French . . . not brown . . . not Jeb. Still, my heart races as I watch the old man struggling for life.

Holding gauze to his abdomen where guts protrude through his ribs, the medics wheel the soldier straight to the surgery unit.

"He hasn't a dog's chance of making it, Stubby." Barney sadly rubs my ear as we watch.

Toward dawn, a loud moan wakes me. The French soldier is back. His cot has been wheeled to the side, and a solemn-faced doctor stands by his side.

"We've done all we can, sir," the doctor whispers quietly to the Frenchman. "It's in God's hands now."

"*Mais non!*" The patient moans. "*Je veux vivre!* I want to live! I want to see my wife! My children. Help me, doctor!" He grabs the doctor's hand. "You must fix me! Get me well!"

The doctor's sad eyes are his answer. He pulls away from the soldier's thin fingers and pats the man's arm. "Be patient . . . and pray."

All-day, between moans, the old man cries out in a mantra: "I will get well. I will see my wife. I will see my children."

As the ether wears off, his eyebrows knot in vicious pain. A somber-faced nurse brings him morphine. Yet still, he cries: "I will get well! I will see my children!"

All day, I watch from under Barney's cot – and will the Frenchman to stay strong.

Close to dinner time, a General in a sharp French uniform comes in. He has no sword, just a riding-whip, which he tosses on the bed. His face is stoic, his eyes showing no feeling as he walks to the old soldier's bed. The soldier's eyes are closed.

"Caporal Bernard Maison, in the name of the Republic of France, I confer upon you the *Medaille Militaire*." The General bends over and kisses the soldier's forehead. He pins the medal to the sheet and departs.

The Caporal Maison jerks his head toward the General's back; his eyes are fierce, his breathing weak.

"I don't want your medal!" He coughs. "I know what this means. I've seen these things before. You've given up! You think I'm gonna die!" His head falls back on the pillow. "I'm not gonna die! I'm gonna see my family. I'm telling you ... I'm going to see my family...."

He moans again and closes his eyes. Soon his chest slowly settles into a faint rise and fall of sleep. His arm drops from the cot to the floor.

I crawl quietly over to the soldier's cot and lie by his hand, nuzzling under it until it lies on my neck.

Hours later, the soldier awakens, clutched in pain. His hand clenches into a fist, pinching my hide. I wriggle free.

"*Je ne tiens plus!*" His cries are desperate. "I can't go on. Have mercy! The pain!"

In response, Nurse Borg comes over with an IV. The pungent scent of antiseptic joins the rank mix of alcohol and infection. "I'll call the priest," she says softly.

The Priest? No! I can't let him give up!

Gently, I lick the soldier's hand and whimper softly. In the distance, I hear the thunder of gunfire. More wounded. More heroes. *But this one, this one has to make it!*

As the morphine dulls the pain, his fist relaxes, and child-like tears roll down his cheeks and wet the sheet above me. "My boy . . . he has a dog, too." The soldier's voice is faint. I lick his hand, trying to encourage him.

The door opens, and I back under the soldier's cot as

a Priest enters. Through the open door, I see distant fields; I smell the fresh-cut hay.

The Priest holds a tray of bottles. Caporal Maison does not accept the Priest's comfort but turns his face to the wall. "I want to live," he repeats in a dwindling voice.

The Priest whispers softly to the soldier.

"I want to live," the soldier answers.

The Priest implores again, in a whisper. He dips his finger in one of the bottles and touches the oil to the top and sides of the soldier's face.

"I want to live!" the soldier sobs in response. Finally, the soldier surrenders and murmurs low words to the Priest.

The Priest whispers a prayer and departs.

I crawl out from my hiding spot and lick the Caporal Maison's hand. He strains his neck down, and I meet his gaze.

"My boy," he whispers. "His name is Orville."

I blink my understanding and lick his hand. He closes his eyes, and I crawl back over to Barney.

"Too bad, buddy," says Barney softly. "He won't make it through the night. I heard the Doc tell Nurse Borg. Too bad, too. He was a brave soldier." He scratches my back, and we lie and watch the old soldier's troubled breathing.

Barney's breathing settles into the deep rhythm of sleep, and I creep over to the French man's bed. I hop up and quietly curl against his side.

Brave soldier, my heart pleads, *please make it*.

Feverish gasps and coughs wake me before dawn.

Caporal Maison! He's still alive! I squirm around and lick his hand, and yip softly.

"Out of the way!" Nurse Borg's voice is harsh as she

shoos me off the cot. Quickly, she grabs a pan and rolls Maison on his side. Vomit splats in the pan, and the stench nauseates me. I jump down and retreat to Barney's bunk.

"How about that!" says Barney. "He sure showed them." His voice lowers. "He made it through the night anyway."

The doctor comes in, and Nurse Borg calls him over. He takes his stethoscope, listens to Maison's heart, and meets the nurse's eyes.

"I don't believe it," he says. "His heart and pulse are stronger. You can write this one down as a miracle."

A miracle. And a real hero will make it home to see his boy.

On my pallet, I lick my paw. *Will I be a brave soldier? Will I make it back to Conroy?*

PART FOUR - Devil Dogs

20

My own healing takes six weeks, according to Conroy, when he finally comes back and gets me from the hospital. It seems like forever. I yip and jump in circles. I run from Conroy to Sam to Ellis and lick them, eager to get their scratches and hugs. I'm happy to be back with my boys.

I rejoin the Yankee Division at a small town that Conroy calls Chateau Thierry. It sits right on the edge of a river. "Marne River," the Captain calls it. A stone bridge spans the river to more buildings on the other side.

"River? We call that a creek back at my home," quips Ellis.

"Big enough for our purposes," says the Captain. "The other side is held by the Germans. Let's keep them on that side."

We pull back to a tiny village consisting of a church and a few small houses and make camp. Our line of trenches lies between the town and our dugouts. The scents are familiar – the muddy clothes and latrines and sulfur and gun powder – and rats. I settle back into the trench routine.

"Dang!" growls Sam, slapping and scratching at the back of his neck.

"What's wrong?" Ellis takes a swig of water from his canteen.

"Dang cooties!" sputters Sam. "I've gotta cut down on my eating."

"What do you mean?" Ellis scratches his head. "You're skin and bones as it is."

"Yeah, but the more I eat, the fatter these buggers get!"

Ellis snorts, and water sprays out his nose.

Charlie chuckles, and even Captain Rous cracks a grin.

My side suddenly itches: I lift my right hind leg and scratch it.

"We've missed you, Stubby, but we've been having the time of our life," says Ellis. He wipes his face and then gives me an excellent welcome-back rub down. "Life of luxury living underground with all the cooties and the rats."

Rats! My nose twitches, and my eyes shoot around. *I'm back with my pack -- and the rats!*

"C'mon, Stubby." Conroy wakes me in the night. A rare moon peeks between the clouds. "We're on patrol."

But instead of heading to the trenches, Conroy, Ellis, Sam, and the Captain march toward the river. A high bank rises on our side, a steep slope sliding toward the river on the other. It proves difficult for my boys to scale, but I scratch to the top with no problem.

As we peek over the top, something whizzes by my head, and I flatten to the ground. I hear Conroy flop down beside me. We wait as another shell bites the dirt beside us. Like a crab, Conroy crawls his way back down. We creep back down our hill, dropping to the ground with each whizz of a shell.

The Captain sends Sam back for a machine-gunner, and Conroy and I scout the scrub on the hilltop for a covered spot to set up the gun.

Our gun is in place by midnight, but the shelling has stopped. From the thicket, we peer across the river. I lift my head and breathe in. Water, grass, deer scat. I look to Conroy. His look reminds me to stay put.

Smoke from smudge fires wafts over the river, carried by a gentle breeze.

I sniff – and sneeze! I bark the alarm. *Gas*! I run around the boys, barking wildly. *Gas*!

"Hush! Stubby!" barks Conroy. "What's wrong with you?"

I *yelp*! and leap around Conroy, pulling at his pant leg.

"Stubby! What's your problem?"

I dart over to the side and bury my nose under a blanket. Bury my nose, then my head, then my chest – until only my rump and stub of a tail stick out.

"Oh, my God!" yells Conroy. "It's gas! Gas! Men! Get your masks!"

From under the covers, I hear the boys mumble through their masks.

"There it is! There's the cloud!"

"Making us mask up," says Conroy. "Old Fritz knows we can't see as well through these masks." He reaches under the blanket and buckles mine around my neck.

Suited and ready, my boys wait and watch the sky. But the yellow smoke cloud hovers in the middle of the river. Then slowly, very slowly, it drifts back toward the German bank.

"Glory be!" yells Ellis. "The wind's changing. Look!

The smoke and gas go rolling up the hill over the enemy lines. We pull off our masks and breathe clean air.

"Whoo, boy!" says Sam. "Now let *them* sniff that stuff awhile."

The river clears in just a few minutes, and we see the enemy troops scurrying about, looking for cover. Sam takes aim with the machine gun.

Rat-a-tat-tat-tat! Our machine gunners begin flattening the soldiers.

"Guess they know whose side God's on now!" Ellis yells over the firing.

The Germans try to fight back but cower under the barrage of gunfire.

I weave among the other soldiers who have joined our battle, making my way down the shore, scouting for the enemy. Then I race back to Conroy.

"*C'mon*!" I bark. I dart back and forth, coaxing Conroy to follow me. He understands and calls a couple of others to come with him.

I run to my lookout point, stop, bark, and point with my nose. Conroy scans the river.

"There!" he calls out. "They're crossing the river! Bye, Golly! They're tying their boats together! Making a bridge. Quick, guys, get 'em!"

As if in answer, a French shell arcs overhead and lands among the boats.

Boom! A burst of water and smoke erupts. When the smoke clears, the boats and soldiers have disappeared. A few rough planks float in the river.

Before daybreak, the Germans try to cross the river on boat bridges twice more. Each time our Doughboys and the French answer with deadly firepower.

Seeing this won't work, the Germans try to paddle across. Again, our machine gunners pelt the men with fire and shoot holes in the boats. Desperate soldiers dive into the river and try to swim ashore. Our soldiers pull them out and take them as prisoners.

Before noon the German guns are silent. We begin trudging back toward camp for some much-needed chow. We dodge limbs blown from treetops and shell holes pocking the field. Not even a rabbit peeks through the scarred area but instead hides in deep holes, safe from the human fighting.

Back at camp, I scarf down the chow that Conroy shares with me and lie down at his feet. Very soon, I drift off and dream of the rabbits.

Reveille blares too soon. But Conroy has a surprise after breakfast.

"Come on, Partner. We're going for a bath."

He and several of the boys trot down the riverbank, away from the houses and out of sight of the German camp. Then they strip. They stand for a moment and laugh at their lily-white butts, then yell and charge into the river. I dash after them.

Some of them squeal like little girls in the icy water. Others dive under and comb their hands through their hair, raking out the mud and blood and lice. Climbing back out, they quickly dry off and pull on their clothes. I give my butt a good shake and spray water all over Conroy's dry shirt. He chases me up the hill.

He stops.

"Hey!" I follow his eyes up the hill and see a half-dozen kids peeking over the top and giggling.

"Hey, kids!" he calls. More giggles follow, and the kids duck and bolt like scared rabbits down the hill and out of sight.

While Conroy works on his gear in the afternoon, I venture back into the village. Our soldiers have been here before, and the villagers welcome them, especially the children, who play with American soldiers. The kids chatter in French, which our boys don't understand, but that doesn't stop them from having fun. A child says, "hello," which is all the English he knows, and the soldier is instantly won over. One soldier rigs a makeshift seesaw out of planks and a barrel: another soldier nails back together a bench blown apart by shells. Another helps rehang a door, and several play games of catch with a ball.

When he's ready to go, the soldier says the one word he knows of French: "*Fee-neesh.*" Then the soldier and child share a smile and go their separate ways.

I stay a little longer – because the kids look good for a game of fetch and a good back scratch, and maybe even a bite of biscuit.

As the sun drops behind the trees, I turn toward camp.

"*Chiot! Venez!*" A young boy, whom the other kids call Pierre, calls me back. He holds out a hand with a bit of beef.

"*Venez!*" Pierre pulls back the meat and runs off. He stops. Looks back. Calls again. Runs again.

With my mouth drooling for the meat, I take off after

him.

Pierre darts down a side street and up the steps to a small house. He stops at the door and holds his hand back toward me.

"*Maman!*" he calls into the house. "*Maman! J'ai apporté le chiot!*"

"*Bon!*" Pierre's mother steps out the door.

"*Venez, chiot.*" She stoops and speaks softly. She takes the piece of beef from Pierre and holds it out in her hand.

I venture forward and sniff her hand. With a smooth slide of my tongue, I take the meat and lick her fingers. Cooing soft words, she gently rubs my back. She turns and whispers to Pierre. He slips into the house and returns quickly with a piece of brightly decorated chamois blanket.

"*Mon héro,*" she says softly as she and Pierre tie the blanket on my back.

Pierre touches each of the colored patches.

"*Les drapeaux,*" he says, with pride. "*Les drapeaux des alliés.*"

The blanket feels strange, like it's not supposed to be there. I shake, but it doesn't come off. I curl around, but I can't get it in my teeth. I spin in a circle. I can't get it. I sit and scratch at it with my front paw. It stays put. I stand on three legs and paw at it with my hindfoot. Nothing.

Pierre laughs and tugs it straight. He pats my back and gives me a good rub, even behind the ears. "*Bon Chien,*" he says. I like his voice. He likes the blanket, I can tell. He pulls out a biscuit from his pocket and offers it to me. After a quick squeeze around my neck, he goes inside and shuts the door.

With a final shake, I turn and head up the street in the direction of the camp.

I *yip!* and dive to the side, barely missed by a cart of firewood barreling out of an alley. I roll over and scrabble back to my paws.

"Stay the hell out of my way, you mongrel!" The voice sends a chill through me.

Billy!

He stops the cart in front of me and pulls out a stick. He slaps it into his fist. His eyes glint with meanness. I recoil, already feeling the blow. But it doesn't come.

"You've got no business around here. Nobody wants you around." He drops the stick into the cart. "I don't care what silly rag some old ladies tie on you. So, you stay away from me, you got it?"

Got it. My insides are trembling; I hold still until he is out of sight.

21

Back at camp, I inch around, keeping an eye out for Billy. His shadow looms long beside the tent. He steps quietly out of sight as Conroy steps out.

"Hey, partner. Where've you been?" Conroy stoops, and I trot over.

"Well, lookie there," says Ellis, joining him. "Stubby's done got himself a cape!"

"Where did you get that?" Conroy fingers the patches on the blanket. If I had lips, I'd tell him. I settle for licking his face.

"Some village ladies must have made it."

"These are the French flags" Conroy traces a design on my back. "Those ladies must like you, fella." Conroy seems pleased, and my heart swells, just a bit.

Trench life trudges on. We battle by day and scout by night. In between, we crouch in the trenches, huddled around a small fire in search of warmth and rest. When they can find a moment, the boys write letters home, play cards, or make up songs. One of them, Sergeant Curtin, writes a poem about me and stuffs it in his helmet; but he showed it to Sam, and now Sam likes to sing it. Conroy thinks it is funny, especially when I howl as Sam sings the last lines: "He always knew when to duck the shells/And buried his nose at the first gas smells."

One night I wake, the hard duckboards of the trenches grating my bones. I sense a menace. *Did I hear something?* I wander among my boys, who are propped against the walls and trying to get some rest, still scratching at the cooties. All look safe, so I scramble over the parapet to scout the area.

"Uhhh . . ." I hear a familiar whispered groan a few yards away. *Someone's injured.* The sound pulls me toward a tall scraggly bush beside our second trench.

Smells American. I creep closer and see the legs of an American uniform sticking out from the hedge.

A second scent mixes in. Sour. Not American.

"*Here, boy. Come here.*" The whispered words sound heavy with a deep-throated accent. Not American. Not French.

German! I peer around the branches. A soldier crouches there, marking on his notepad.

"*Easy. Come here, boy.*" He whispers. He pulls a piece of bread from his pocket and holds it toward me. But he's not one of our boys.

"*Grrrrr . . .*" I pull back my lips in a snarl. My ears fly back. I crouch to leap.

Alarmed, the soldier flees, but I am too fast. I fly up and latch on to his pant leg.

He trips.

Whack! A hard blow to my face jolts loose my grip. He scrambles up and runs.

I charge again.

Snap! I clamp down hard on the German's buttocks. He falls face down under my assault.

"Yeow!" He screams. He pelts my flanks with his fist. But I lock my jaws and hold on.

In the dark, I hear the rapid crunch of boots.

"Stubby? Where are you?"

I growl an answer.

Conroy runs over and aims his rifle at my captive. "Surrender!" he demands. I hang on, with the German still pounding my flank.

"Surrender!" Conroy jabs his rifle butt into the German, knocking him back. He sticks the barrel in his face.

"*Kamerad*," mutters the German.

"I've got him, Partner. Let him go." I obey.

Conroy marches the German back to his camp.

"Hey, look here!" Conroy calls to his buddies. "Ole Stubby has caught himself a German!"

"Woo-Hoo!" Ellis joins Conroy and pins the German's hands behind his back.

Conroy and Sam and Ellis march the spy to the Captain and relate the story of his capture.

"And he had this with him." Conroy hands him a muddy notepad.

"I think your dog's caught himself a spy," says the Captain. "This looks like a diagram of our trenches."

Conroy pats my side, and I get a warm feeling inside.

"Here, I think you've earned this." The Captain takes an Iron Cross off the German's uniform and pins it on my blanket. Conroy's eyes look proud.

"Well, Conroy. What you've got yourself there is a regular four-legged war hero!" Ellis stoops and scruffs my neck.

I straighten my back and lift my chin. I like the sound of that.

"Come on, Stubby." Conroy's summons wakes me from my late afternoon nap. "We have a special mission."

Clouds roll in, covering the moon and hurrying the fast-approaching darkness. Sam and Charlie sling on their backpacks and join us as we hike through camp and head down a path against the bank. Dark holes in the middle of the course remind us of yesterday's shelling. Abandoned haversacks and camp gear lie strewn about from the rushed retreat of the Germans beaten back by our troops.

We tread quietly, hearing only the crunch of the soldiers' boots.

"Stubby, come on." Conroy's call is impatient.

My ears pique, and I stop. I turn my head to the right and emit a low growl.

"What is it, Stubby?" Sam stoops beside me.

"Shhh! Listen," says Conroy.

Tick. Tick. Tick. Their human ears pick up what I have heard.

Sam rises and follows the faint ticks.

"Is that a clock?" He reaches for an ordinary-looking alarm clock lying next to some abandoned gear."

"Don't touch it!" warns Conroy in a half-whisper. "Look. This place was picked clean when they left. Systematically. So, why leave a clock?"

"It's just a clock."

"Maybe. But it might be connected to an explosive. We better leave it alone."

"That sounds smart." Sam backs away from the clock. "Let's not take any chances.

We make a wide circle around the stack of gear and continue our trek.

We come upon a small ditch about a mile farther down the trail. Only occasional bushes and trees dot the bank. Empty monkey meat cans and spent shells suggest some of our boys have camped here earlier. But the strongest scent isn't of the camp.

Following the stench of decay to the top of the ridge, we meet a horrid sight. The hillside is dotted with dead bodies.

We scout among the bodies to look and listen for life, but any survivors have been removed.

As we follow the small ravine, blood spots and burned places on the ground mark where shells have fallen. Our walk becomes silent and solemn as we pass through the battle graveyard.

Grrrr. I bristle and stop, picking up an animal scent. Conroy heeds my alert.

"What is it, boy? What do you hear?"

With a low growl, I take a few steps towards a dugout area ahead of us.

In the opening, a curtain waves in and out with the breeze.

Conroy, Sam, and Charlie hoist their rifles and close in on the dugout.

I follow, alert and ready. Conroy pulls out his pistol.

Cautiously, Conroy pushes aside the curtain with his bayonet and sticks his pistol in the opening.

A loud *Woof!* erupts! A large, yellow mutt charges out of the dugout.

In a flash, I bolt beside Conroy and give a loud snarl, my lips pulled back, baring my teeth.

The mutt freezes with his ears laid flat, head lowered.

His hair is muddy and mangy, his eyes yellowish and bloodshot. His growl is weary. His spindly legs and jutting ribs are covered in burns, sores, and wounds. His tail tucks. I smell his defeat.

"Look at him. That poor dog is starving." Charlie puts down his rifle and stoops. I low-growl a warning.

"It's okay, fella," Charlie speaks softly to the dog. "We're not gonna hurt you." He digs a hunk of bread from his pack. "Here, boy." Keeping his eyes locked on the dog, he places the bread on a flat rock at the bottom of the creek bed.

"Come on," says Conroy. "Let's back away slowly. He's too weak to bother us."

I keep a low growl but follow Conroy's lead. The yellow dog's eyes dart suspiciously from us to the bread and back. When we get farther away, he braves a step forward.

As we turn and regroup with the pack, I steal a look back and see the dog snapping up the bread like a hungry gull after a minnow.

As we come to the edge of the woods, we spot a cabin across a pocked field of tall grass. We keep in the cover of the woods and circle the area.

We pass a shell hole about as wide as Conroy is tall. It's filled partially with muddy water. Lying half in it are two dead German soldiers – and a dead mule. Maggots crawl out of the mule's flesh. The stench of rotting flesh is suffocating. I shake my head to clear my nose and dart around the scene for some fresher air.

The cabin sits nestled under some trees. A Captain comes out to meet us. Without a word, Conroy hands him a folded message, which the Captain unfolds and reads.

"Is there an answer, sir?"

"Yes, one moment." The Captain disappears back inside the cabin. A moment later, he returns and hands Conroy another folded message.

"You'd better hurry back," the Captain says, then turns and reenters the cabin.

We retrace our steps, making a wider circle to avoid the shell hole with the mule.

We find no sign of the yellow dog.

STUBBY'S WAR

22

As the rains resume, we're on the move again. We trudge through the mud. Elbow to elbow, we pack into trucks and slop through the hills and valleys.

"Belieau Wood," Conroy announces as we spill out of the trucks.

"Forest of Horror," Sam whispers. "That's what they call it."

Dark, naked trunks stretch to the sky like skeletons. I skirt around one and relieve myself. Huge boulders lie strewn like bodies among broken trunks and limbs.

"What's that?" Ellis points ahead to a round brick structure about as tall as four of my boys. Arched windows look out from different sides.

"Maison." The Captain answers. With his knife, he scrapes mud from the sole of his boot. "Built as a shelter for hunters, but today it's a lookout for us.

As we get nearer, I catch the scent of Germans. With

a sharp bark, I tear out for the door.

"Stubby, wait!" I hear Conroy, but I'm already at the door.

Woof! I answer back.

"Spread out!" the Captain orders.

Conroy and Ellis drop to the left, bodies flat against the wall. Sam and Billy flank out on the other side. I keep my post in front.

Conroy and Sam charge the door with a silent count of three, guns drawn. I dart in behind.

The stench of death is pungent. Seven Germans inside, all dead. Their mangled bodies litter the entrance, some still clutching their guns. I follow Sam's gaze upward. Like a giant monster bite, the shelter's back wall gapes open.

"Helluva fight here," says Sam.

"And not over yet." The Captain's voice calls from the doorway. "Let's go find our men."

Our soldiers have billeted in small dugouts near the front, behind the trenches. A dozen men in each hole. Dirt and dead bushes cover their hideouts, held up by iron sheets.

We pick our way quietly forward. Closer in, a platoon of boys 'digs in.' Each man has dug his own hole in the ground, large and deep enough for one. Like the bigger dugouts, these are covered with dirt and bushes.

Some are not hidden well enough, though. Those that were spotted by the enemy now scar the woods as gaping graves.

All around us, weapons thunder. The *rat-tat-tat* of machine guns echoes our footsteps as Conroy and I trudge through the battle-worn forest. Shells fly around us. Dead horses lie everywhere. Cool forest scents are blasted away, replaced by whiffs of sulfur, gunpowder, and sad decay.

With big red crosses painted on their sides, Ambulances belch gas fumes as they lumber down the muddy paths carting our wounded to safety.

Above the rumble of the ambulance engines, I hear another roar getting louder and louder. I look up as a giant bird glitters in the sun, growing larger and larger.

"Take cover!" Conroy and the boys fall flat beneath the trees.

Boom!

The ground erupts. I drop flat and hear dull thuds around me as soldiers fall, groaning, spouting blood -- whole limbs severed. Frantic horses break loose and run.

Two more explosions follow as my boys take cover under the bushes. Trembling, I press against Conroy and try to buck up. He gives me a quick pat on the shoulder but keeps his eyes peeled on the battle scene.

The roar of the metal bird grows distant . . . then all is silent.

I scrabble up. My boys are safe, but all around us, clutching sides and legs and heads, lie desperate, wounded soldiers.

Sam runs to a young fellow lying nearby. Blood spurts from the boy's leg. Sam unbuckles the boy's belt and cinches it around the leg.

"Get a medic!"

Conroy and I take off toward the ambulance line.

Woof! I jerk to a stop.

Conroy stops, hears the whine, and looks up as a shell arcs over us.

"Gas!" Conroy drops to the ground and pulls on his mask. He grabs me and holds mine tightly against my face. We huddle until the shell hits, then, crouching low, we make our way to the ambulance.

Other wounded soldiers call as we pass. Their faces contort in pain, pale as ashes.

"Water. Help me, please...."

I want to stay and help, but I stay close to Conroy.

We hail the medic, who grabs an aide and follows us.

We find Sam still applying pressure to the young soldier's wound. He has managed to staunch the bleeding. With his free hand, he holds the soldier's gas mask over his mouth.

His own mask hangs loosely around his neck.

"Take him." Sam's voice croaks. His eyes roll back, and he falls to the side of the bleeding soldier.

"I've got this one. You get Sam!" The medic grabs the bleeding leg.

"Sam!" yells Conroy. "Billy! Help me! It's Sam!"

Conroy loops his arms under Sam's shoulders. Billy grabs his feet, and they carry him toward the ambulance.

As I follow across the field, I see two men die right before my eyes, too late for any help.

Hang in there, Sam. We're getting help. Hang in there.

A rapid clip-clop of hooves snaps my attention. I half-turn then dive behind a tree, barely escaping a wild-eyed wounded horse squealing and galloping past. An image of being trampled under the hooves shudders through me.

Hunkered down, I pick up a new scent – distress. I spot a young chestnut mare at the edge of the path, tethered to a tree, tugging at the ropes. Flecks of pain cross her half-closed eyes. Blood drips steadily from a hole in her side, draining her life. Her whinnying grows weaker and weaker.

Nearby, Ellis helps a wounded soldier to stand. I rush over, barking urgently, and tug at his pant leg. He gets the message and follows me to the chestnut. Sadness darkens his eyes.

"I'll handle this, Stubby. You go on back."

Conroy whistles, and I run back to him.

Moments later, I hear the solitary burst of a pistol shot and know the mare's suffering is ended.

As sleep finally comes in the evening, my tired paws twitch and jerk to images of the day's horror. The shelling. The wounded. Sam. The wild horse. The mare. *Sam.*

STUBBY'S WAR

23

Scritch. Scritch. Scritch.

A scratching drags me back from my fitful sleep. The moon peeks from the clouds and casts shadows over the forest floor. I quietly crawl out of our pup tent and investigate.

Among the shadows, the scene is grim – black ruins from the day's battle silhouetting against the sky. But the floor of the scene is alive with tiny, skittering forms. I sniff the air.

Rats! I silently lick back the involuntary drool. *Control yourself.* A chase will wake not only my sleeping comrades but also any Fritz camped nearby.

I shrink back into the shadows and watch.

Rats are everywhere, darting from rock to rock, scuffling with each other, scavenging any morsels of meat or bread left by the humans. My ears twitch and my fur bristles, but I crouch in silence.

I sense more eyes watching the scene and spot two glittering eyes in the dark limbs of a treetop.

A shadow briefly flits over the moon, and with a sudden *whoosh* of wings, a great barn owl descends and snatches up a victim.

A tiny screech of pain erupts, and rats scatter to dark holes and hideaways. Silently, the owl and his prey disappear into the trees.

Conroy wakes my pack at dawn. I dart around, checking on my boys – Conroy...Ellis...Charlie... *Sam?*

I drop my head to my paws and look up at Conroy.

"I know, fellow. You miss him, don't you?" He kneels beside me. "Sam'll be all right." He gently pats my side. He lets out a long sigh. "War is hell." He stands. "Come on, partner."

We head out but not toward the front. We have a message to deliver to the back – to the tank brigade.

As I trot along, I breathe in woodland scents free of the blood and gunpowder of the day before. Birds chitter, squirrels dart among the treetops, and an occasional deer silently flicks its ears and chews the tips of branches. I sniff and listen but keep my place next to Conroy.

We break into a clearing and find gleaming metal tanks – giant, hulking turtles on tracks. Scurrying among the tanks, soldiers, some stripped to the waist, service the guns, check the ammo, and fire test rounds with speed and precision. Odors of sweat and gunpowder crowd out the woodland scents.

"Ain't this the life," snorts Ellis as he greets one of

the soldiers. "We're upfront being chewed up and stopping bullets, and you guys are back here running around shirtless and picnicking."

"Yeah? Well, you Doughboys can g'wan back to where you come from. Our chiefs tell us if we're still alive in a week, they'll kill us themselves," retorts a gunner. But they both laugh, and the gunner offers to show us around.

Thin and wiry, the soldier wipes his face with a greasy rag, adding black smears to the ones already there. His fingernails and creases are filled with black. He smells of mud and motor oil.

We wander around the field and see a gaggle of different tanks – giant monster turtles on notched tracks. Our guide calls some of them "whippets" and some "baby" tanks, but they all look huge to me. He calls some "male" and some "female," but how can he tell?

"They're different for doing different jobs," the gunner explains. He pats one as if it's a pet. He points out the canopy of limbs and bushes under which most of the tanks are parked.

"That's to keep Ole Fritz's pilots guessing where we're keeping them," he says. "They'd give their eye teeth to be able to knock these all out with one swipe."

He directs Conroy to a tent deeper in the woods. "Come on," he says. "I know you've got some news. Since they've been collecting all these babies together, I know something big is about to happen."

Back in the trench, the hours drag by. We wait for the order to attack. The clouds hide the moon as we scan the battlefield ahead. The air is gray and chilly.

A monotonous hum breaks the silence; then, the

murmur erupts into a grind. Something's coming. I jump up and emit a low growl. I'm alert in all my muscles and even the hair along my back.

"Easy, boy," soothes Conroy as he rubs my neck. "They're on our side."

Three huge turtle-tanks, grunting and snorting, creep out of the woods to our rear. I keep guard, my shoulders and back tense, ready.

From the flanks, we watch the assault of the gray monsters as they plod slowly across No Man's Land.

"Come on, boy," signals Conroy. Like a wake behind a ship, my boys fall in behind the tanks and march toward the enemy lines.

Only the tanks' heavy breathing breaks the silence. On we march. So far, no thunder from enemy guns. Have we caught Ole Fritz asleep? Have they seen our monsters and fled?

Nearer and nearer, we march.

With a grinding screech of metal on metal, barbed-wire entanglements are uprooted and flattened like briars under boots.

The surprise is complete. The assault is on!

With whoops and yells, our artillery fires a barrage of gunfire. The enemy awakes. Hordes of *Boche* uniforms pour from the trenches like a swarm of bees, shouting, yelling, their faces white with fear. Our machine gunners cut them down. We hear the *flap, flap, flap* of bullets meeting flesh as they fall.

But our boys fall, too, to our left and right. Many scream with pain. Others are killed instantly; some are shot eight to ten times before their bodies hit the mud. Bodies lie torn apart. Helmets, arms, and legs litter the battlefield. One soldier nearby spins and falls flat, his vacant eyes staring up at me.

Ellis turns to the side and vomits, heaving onto the mud.

We press on.

We lay a crushing blow on the Germans, but they don't give up.

The enemy soldiers run helter-skelter like ants in a kicked-up ant hill. They fire back as they search for shelter to regroup, but there is nowhere to hide. The monsters crush everything in their path, lumbering down and up in the trenches, plowing down small trees, and flattening enemy guns.

The tanks thunder on.

Out of the ground, ten yards away, an infantryman rises up and waves his rifle furiously.

The lead tank stops. The soldier runs forward. "Look out! Jerry tanks coming!" The soldier drops back into the trench.

"More tanks. German tanks! They're coming!" Ellis echoes the warning, and the word is passed through the lines. I herd my boys toward cover.

Up ahead, a round, squat-looking turtle-monster is advancing. Behind it waves of infantry swarm toward us. Another armed turtle crawls out from the left. A third moves in from the right.

Our turtle monsters plow forward, a giant wall of steel, skirting the trenches and devouring everything in their path. We march behind.

The lead tank stops and rotates left. The gunner – peering through his narrow slit – takes aim and fires.

He misses, overshooting his target, his shell bursting in the dirt. The Germans don't answer. He shoots again, this time hitting to the right of the target. Again, no answer.

A sudden hurricane of bullets hails against our steel wall. We drop for cover.

Above the roar of our engines, I hear the *rat-tat-tat-tat* of machine guns shot – the ping, ping, ping of bullets bouncing off the turtle shell. We huddle behind.

Our turtle-monsters answer with our own armor-piercing shells! As the monster begins to move, my boys duck into a dip in the ground.

Another monster tank grinds by. I jump up beside it. I glare at the enemy.

My blood boils. The beast erupts within me. I want to attack, fight with the monsters, and draw blood. I lunge forward – and choke as I'm yanked back by my collar and roll across the mud.

I growl and snap, struggling to get free of the arms binding me. *Let me at the enemy!*

"Easy, boy." I hear a faint voice through the explosion of shells. "Come on, boy. You stay with me."

With one arm still around me, Conroy crawls backward like a lobster into the ditch with the other boys. My arms and legs tremble. My heart pounds. I gulp the air. Conroy's whispers calm me.

The monster within recedes. The fear creeps back in.

Crouched for cover, we watch -- like spectators -- the battle of machine against machine.

Our tanks maneuver to the left. The field is heavily scarred with shell holes, and the tanks go up and down like ships in a stormy sea, making shooting difficult. Some shots fall short. The next ones overshoot their target.

Voomp! Voomp! Black shell holes spurt from the sides of two of our tanks, and they slowly limp toward the rear.

Twisting and turning, most of our other tanks dodge the enemy shelling. Still, some come dangerously close to our own trenches.

We continue to huddle – and watch. Then a vast figure rises overhead, casting a dark shadow.

I *yelp*! a warning and lunge for the far end of the hole.

My boys join me, waving arms and yelling at the top of their lungs. A giant tank looms above us, about to crash in.

At the last second, the monster tank turns and lumbers back toward its target.

Sounds rattle in my head -- the roar of our tank, the rat-tat-tat of machine guns, and the thunderous boom of tank shells. Gasoline and mud and gun powder scents mingle together and burn my nose.

I crawl over and flatten my body against Conroy. His heart races. Mine races faster. We huddle and wait for orders.

Our front tank-monster fires and explodes the ground right in front of the enemy tank. It adjusts and takes dead aim.

Bwoom!

The turret on top of the German tank explodes, and the tank jolts to a stop. Our tank fires again. A hit. White puffs of smoke belch the front of the tank. A third shell fired. A third hit. The tank keels over to one side. A door opens, and the crew bursts for the trees.

We have killed the monster!

But the German infantry still advances like millions of ants.

Our tanks rain down a volley of shells at the coming soldiers. They scatter for cover.

Then our Captain yells the order.

"Fix bayonets!"

The clang of metal against metal is dulled by another roar from above. I bark to Conroy, but he has heard it, too.

A giant grey bird soars overhead, a large black cross on each underwing. It dives lower and crosses over us. I see the figures of two men in the cockpit.

From the bottom of the bird falls something round and black, like a giant egg. I watch it for a fraction of a second, my chest knotted! I *yelp!* *Take cover!* I pull on Conroy's boot.

A geyser of dirt explodes in the ground in front of our turtle tank. The front tank rears like a giant horse.

Everything shakes and rattles. The engine coughs. *Bam!* It falls back with a crash.

It sits deadly still.

The tank's pillbox on top clangs open. A soldier climbs onto the front and sits astride the cannon, like on a horse, his back still and straight. He points forward and yells a command.

The monster sputters and snorts. It roars back to life and grinds again across the field toward the infantry.

"Dang! Look at that!" Ellis yells over the din. "That's Lieutenant Colonel George Patton!"

Conroy and my boys rise to follow the mounted tank.

"Wait!" barks Captain Rous.

In the distance, I hear another engine roar — higher-pitched than the big one in front of us.

"Look!" Conroy points to seven smaller, faster tanks rolling in toward us.

"Woo-Hoo! Whippets!" says Ellis. "These speed babies will make short work of old Fritz!"

"*Woo-Hoo!*" I bark, my body a-quiver with excitement. *It's about time they bring out the little dogs to mop up this battle.*

I start scratching out to join them, but Conroy grabs my collar and pulls me back.

"Not yet, boy," he says. "Not yet."

We watch. The whippets head straight for the German infantry.

With their turrets on top, the whippets look more like creeping crickets than turtles. They weave and fire their machine guns and cannons at the approaching Fritz. Soldiers scatter. The whippets punch straight into the middle of them, running over them, grinding them under their tracks, and spitting fire as the soldiers retreat.

The whippet work is soon over.

"Nipped in the bud," says Ellis. "We nipped it in the bud."

"Yeah," says Charlie. "But look." I look out over the hole.

Only three of our little tanks, their engines choking and spitting, limp back out of the seven that entered the battle. Four whippets lie silent across the field, smoke puffing from their sides.

24

When the gray dawn breaks through the inky dark, I creep out of the trench and shoot a swift glance across the barren field. Corpses litter the scene like twisted, fallen logs. All is silent. No early morning birds or even scurrying mice. I snuffle along the area to the shell-pocked road. The right leads to the front, to the farthest boundary of yesterday's hard-earned territory.

I turn left.

I trot on to clear my nose of the scents of death and gunpowder until I, at last, inhale the sweet smell of pine. Faint chirps and twitters hint at life among the branches.

A lone figure materializes before me, limping on a crutch made from a broken branch. In familiar khaki and green, a wounded soldier stumbles forward in the middle of the road. But it's the wrong way! He needs to go back. To the medics.

As I near the soldier coated in dirt and blood from

his face to his boots, I bark recognition. *Billy! And Billy is hurt.*

"Get away! Get away from me!" His voice slurs the words. His face is pale, eyes rolling uncontrolled from side to side. He holds one leg up, heaving and panting with each step. Canvas strips, unwound from his injured leg, drag the ground as he moves forward.

I try to rub his leg, but he pushes me away with his stick.

In the distance behind me, I hear the rumble of the ambulance truck coming from the front. Billy's got to get off the road!

With my teeth, I grab the hanging strip and pull him toward the side of the road.

"Let me go!" He hops forward, dragging me several paces. He jerks the strip from my mouth. I bark and grab it frantically.

"Let me go, you mongrel!" He swings his stick crutch like a club and slams my head.

White light flashes in my head, matched with a deafening roar of thunder. My legs collapse. I fall. I try to stand. The air fights against me. I try again. Groans of pain rumble from deep in my chest. With another twist, I manage to stand up. I *yelp* as pain screeches through my head.

Through a blur, I see Billy still stumbling in the middle of the road. The ambulance truck grows larger and louder. He doesn't hear it – or doesn't care.

I snap around in front of Billy. His face is pasty, his eyes rolling wildly. I push on his legs, pushing him toward the edge. He spins and trips a few feet to the side. I push again. He shuffles a few feet more. His hand reaches out for a tree trunk. His eyes widen at the touch. He stumbles over the roots to the far side and slumps to the ground.

The ambulance rumbles past.

Billy's head lolls to the side, and he spots me.

"What you doing here, you danged mongrel?" He pants heavily. Cautiously, I nuzzle his leg. This time he doesn't push me aside.

"I shoulda known. Go on. Get outta here." His voice is a shaky whisper. I rub against his side. His head rolls to the other side and back toward me. His face winces in racking pain. With his eyes closed, he groans and coughs. His hand drops down, and I feel one finger moving back and forth on my neck. I draw the metallic scent of blood across my nostrils.

I whine and push his face with my nose. He looks down and then drops his head back on the trunk.

"My leg." His breathing comes in labored huffs when he talks, like a desperate half-whisper. "I can't feel my leg." He pushes back his coat and studies his thigh and uniform soaked in blood. His chest looks like it's been chewed by wolves.

"But, hell! I can feel my gut! Old Fritz done got me good." He chokes out a sort of half-laugh. With a heavy groan, he closes his eyes. I lie still, resting my head on his leg.

Finally, his chest heaves again. "Still here, fleabag? You waitin' on me, you're out of luck. Not going anywhere any time soon."

He struggles to breathe and lets out a moan.

"You crazy dog." I work my nose under his arm and whine softly. He offers a grim smile, cracking the mud on his face.

"Had a dog once," His face contorts with pain. "Mutt like you. Littler, though. But he was my buddy. What I called him – Buddy."

I lick his chin and meet his eyes.

"Dad comes in drunk one night." He pauses to get his breath. "Laid into me with his belt." He inhales. His eyes squeeze shut. After a moment, he looks at me. "Buddy couldn't stand it. Growled ... flew up ..."

A fit of coughing stops him. He shudders and drops his head back and closes his eyes. I stay tight against him. *I'll keep him warm. The medic will come.*

His head rolls to the side, and he sleeps. His jaw drops open. His breaths grow fainter and fainter. Then he is still. My heart is sad as I close my eyes at the scent of death.

The crunch of boots stirs me awake. I spring up and *woof* a call.

"There they are!" calls Conroy. "Stubby!" He breaks into a run toward us. Charlie is right behind him. They stoop and inspect Billy. Conroy squeezes his eyes shut and looks away.

"Stubby," Conroy whispers. "You found Billy. You stayed with him, didn't you, boy? Stayed with him till the end."

I exhale with a whimper, needing Conroy's touch. He stays on his knee for a long minute, removing his helmet and, with the back of his fist, rubs his eye. Charlie, too, removes his helmet and drops his head.

With a deep inhale, Conroy stands.

"Come on, partner. Let's go clean up that head of yours. Looks like you got hit."

Silently, I follow him back to camp, leaving Billy.

25

The rains resume, and we trudge through the dark woods. No lights allowed. Rain soaks through the soldiers' coats and rolls off my fur. Fog worsens visibility. Conroy attaches a leash to my collar, and I lead him through the underbrush. Together we guide the other boys as each keeps one hand on the pack of the boy ahead. We hike for about a half-mile to an open field and wait for orders.

"St. Mihiel," the Captain announces. "Zero hour."

We gaze ahead. As far as we can see, sheets of flame flash from the artillery. The earth quakes. In the distance, fires blaze from villages, haystacks, and ammunition dumps.

"They're retreating, but they're burning everything in their path," says the Captain. "Destroying everything."

Coming from the battlefront, slump-shouldered German prisoners file past us, under the guard of French and British units. Steady streams of our own men and wagons of weapons and supplies pass us from behind, headed toward the front.

We make camp.

Before dawn, an explosion rocks the earth and lights up the skies. The front line roars and crashes as American turtle-monsters pound the battleground, ripping enemy barbed wire into shreds, caving in trenches, and eliminating machine-gun holes.

"Softening them up for us." Conroy clicks his bayonet in place.

Our tanks and infantry have the enemy in retreat. We have mop-up duty.

Conroy signals, and we lead the boys across a landscape pocked with shell craters, smashed and burning haystacks, and bodies of fallen soldiers. Familiar odors of gunpowder, burning hay, decay, and fresh blood mingle in the haze of the battlefield.

Overhead, I see the metal birds and bark at Conroy, but he says they are ours, patrolling for the enemy.

The roads are busy with the bustle of soldiers no longer concerned with hiding. Now wagon trains, truck convoys, artillery, tanks, and dozens of ambulances with their loads of wounded soldiers dodge the shell holes and jam the roads.

More enemy soldiers file past, herded by Doughboys and French military police. Some captives look relieved to be out of battle.

"They know we'll take care of them," says Conroy, "even if they are the enemy."

We make our way down into a valley.

"Woohoo! Would ya look at this?" calls Ellis.

"*Woo hoo!*" I howl. The scene before us is nothing like the devastation we have just crossed.

"This must have been their headquarters," says Conroy as we make our way down the hill. "Looks like the officer's camp."

Instead of sandbags and duckboards, the trenches here are dotted with concrete dugouts with bathrooms and hot water – even electric lights are strung up in what looks like officer barracks. In a protected area, pavilions cover rustic tables.

"And look at this food," says Ellis. "Officers sure eat better than us."

Instead of "monkey meat" and stale bread like my boys eat, these Germans have been eating real vegetables and real meat – chicken and pork and – rabbit! Conroy names the source of the sour smell, too – *sauerkraut*. I leave that stuff alone.

My mouth drools at the meat as I take a whiff of what the Germans abandoned in their retreat.

"What'd say we have a snack?" Ellis grabs up a loaf of bread.

We eat like savage wolves, the boys tossing me rabbit and pork pieces they pick off the tables. When our bellies are stuffed, we load up as much grub as we can carry and head back to share it with the rest of the camp. Then, full and content, we rest and wait for our next orders.

Contentment is short-lived, though, and we march to the next battle area during the night. In my boys' faces, the bliss of our feast dims as we march in pouring rain through more devastation with scarred landscapes, burned buildings, and fallen soldiers.

Saddest to me are the horses. Dead horses line the

roadsides, many killed by enemy fire, some still tethered to a wagon or a tree.

"Overwork and exhaustion killed them," says Conroy, his face a mixture of sadness and anger. "Just getting ready for the battle wore them to the bone and sapped their strength."

"Ole Fritz just finished the job." Charlie spits in disgust as we walk past the once-proud steeds.

I remember the mare from the other day. Men and boys are killing the horses. Killing the boys. *Killing Billy*.

Before dawn, we enter the remains of a village and find shelter for the day. Overhead, German planes scout for our soldiers, sometimes swooping down and blasting the roadways to make new holes for us to get around.

Then the planes discover our village.

I huddle out of sight next to Conroy. The planes drop shells around us. The ground erupts. Buildings flatten. In the open streets, more horses die from bullets and shrapnel.

We keep hidden. I weave in and around the legs of my boys, encouraging them – and they encourage me.

Night comes, and my weary boys again plod down the rough road under a rare full moon.

"Tomorrow," they say. "It's coming tomorrow."

26

About the time the sunlight peeks through the branches, we approach the bank of a river. The crisp Fall air tickles my nose. When I scoot off the path to pee, a squirrel overhead shakes pine needles down on my head. Not wanting to lose sight of Conroy, I give the squirrel a quick bark and scurry back to my pack.

"*La Rivière Meuse*," announces the Captain. "We'll rest here today."

"Woo hoo!" says Ellis, dropping his pack. "No fighting today!"

With no rain and a day to rest, it's time to hunt.

I tug at Conroy, and he chases me through a thicket of trees, Ellis close behind. The ground is still wet from yesterday's rain, and I flick little mud bullets behind me as I run. I let Conroy get close, then I turn around and crouch on my front legs, my rear end up in the air. Conroy gets closer, and I spin around and bound up a hill.

I look back to make sure he's following – and suddenly I am slipping, legs spread out like a crab, sliding down the other side – *splat*! into a bowl of mud. I'm surrounded by the mud-slick curves of a shell crater. I spit the dirt from my mouth. The ooze feels soft and cool on my tired legs.

I roll over and coat my fur like mustard on a hot dog. The mud squishes around me and burbles when I pull out my paw.

"Oh......my......gosh." I hear Ellis's voice from the top of the crater.

"Yep," Conroy says. "He's found a mud bath, and he seems to like it, too."

I roll over again, then shake the mud out of my ears.

"Stubby, get back up here!"

I stop mid-frolic to look at Conroy, pulling my lips up in a devilish grin. I turn and try to scamper up the opposite side of the gully. I crab-crawl halfway up and hit an extra slick spot. Then I slide slowly back down, my legs splayed, cold mud chilling my private parts underneath. I *yip*! and try again, digging into the wet soil with my claws.

With mud flying in every direction, I make it to the top, steal a glance back at Conroy, and beeline it down the next hill. I hear Conroy calling me, hear the *clop, clop, clopping* of his boots behind me. Ellis woo-hoos as he follows.

At the river's edge, I don't even slow my pace.

Woof! Splat! I belly flop into the water. I somersault and come up with a gasp for air.

"Woo hoo!" Ellis yells from the top of the rise. "I guess that's one way to get a bath."

"Come on, Stubby. Out of there, now!" Conroy tries to make his voice harsh, but I hear a smile slipping in.

As I begin to shiver, I dog-paddle toward the bank.

"Come on, boy. Let's go find us some grub."

Grub? Food? Oh, yeah!

I bound up the hill and leap for his chest. I make it about as high as his waist, but it's high enough. He topples back on the ground into the mud. I pounce on him and lick his face.

"Okay. Okay. That's enough. Let's go." His voice is harsh like he means it this time.

So, I obey, but not before I give a monster shake from my nose to my tail and rain dog water all over his face.

Then I turn and bolt back to camp.

A couple of days later, I spend the day chasing squirrels. I get back just in time for chow.

"We have a letter from Sam," Conroy announces as I munch my monkey meat. The chow has been better while we've been behind the front line, regrouping. The boys have polished and repaired all their weapons and washed and mended their uniforms. My boys even have new boots. My coat and paws are fine; I just scratch or nibble out any twigs or briars.

"When's Sam comin' back?" Ellis tears off a corner of bread and tosses it my way. He stuffs the rest into his own mouth.

"Not for a while. The doctors won't let him come yet." Conroy scans the letter. "He says there is a group of our Marines there. Got hurt at Belieau Woods, too. Says the Germans have a new word for the Marines – the *Teufel hunden* -- the hell hounds."

"Yeah, they say those Marines have the guts of a bulldog," says Charlie.

Bulldog? I dart my eyes around the room.

"And cold nerve," adds Conroy. "But no more than our boys."

"Yeah, and we got our own Devil Dog!" grunts Ellis. He scratches behind my ear; I wiggle around so he can reach the other one.

Devil Dog! That's me..

27

Conroy, Ellis, and Charlie squat around a small fire, brewing coffee in a tin pot. Two young, fresh-faced newcomers quiz them about their battles. I sense one of them, the skinny one with curly black hair, is a dog lover. I nuzzle his hand and let him scratch my neck.

"Arnie there is from Hartford, and I'm from Boston." The soldier takes a steaming cup from Charlie.

"Connecticut! How 'bout that, Conroy? More Yankees like you!" Ellis slurps loudly as he sips his cup. "So, what are they saying about us back home?"

"They say we're giving the *Boche* a helluva beating! Say we're got him on the run and we're going mop up and be home by Christmas." Arnie accepts a cup.

Ellis snorts coffee out his nose. "By Christmas! Which Christmas? They've been sayin' that for four Christmases now."

"Yeah," mutters Charlie. "Whoever's saying that

doesn't have a clue what it's really like out here."

Stan, the skinny young boy who was petting me, slaps the back of his neck and looks at his hand. "What the heck is this? Fleas?"

"Cooties," says Ellis, "get used to 'em." He flicks a couple of lice off his own sleeve, and the boy scoots a few feet away from him. I feel the need to scratch, so I do.

"So, how many Germans do you think you've killed?" Arnie, the other newcomer, looks from Conroy to Ellis to Charlie. He is short and thick, with muscular arms and short hair that sticks up. "My Pop says to mow them down like tin cans on a log."

"I don't keep count." Charlie's face is solemn, his eyes distant.

"The problem is . . ." Conroy gazes into the fire. "The thing is, there are just as many Germans who think they are going to mow you down like tin cans on a log."

"Well, I'm ready for them." Arnie slaps his thigh. "I'm ready."

"You just watch us." Conroy's voice grows stern. "Do what we do. If we yell *Down!* you flatten your faces to the ground. To hell with being a hero. You hear me?"

The black-haired boy nods, but Arnie keeps his chin up. "I'm not afraid of any Fritz."

"Dreaming is what you're doing," Conroy warns. "And getting yourself killed. Now you watch us, and we'll teach you to stay alive. That's more important than whipping the world."

"Yeah, staying alive," Charlie muses. "If I do, I won't ever worry again. Not a care in the world." He drains the last of his coffee. "If I can make it through this, I can survive anything."

With me following along, Conroy wanders over to the side and leans on the skeleton trunk of a tree. He lights a cigarette, a habit he's picked up in the trench. He places it between his parted lips and sucks in. The acrid odor stings my nose. Ellis joins us under the tree and lights up his own cigarette, but he calls them fags.

"Are you and Charlie trying to scare those boys? This is gonna be their first big battle. We don't need 'em scared before we go." He draws in, and the tip of his cigarette glows.

"We're all scared," Conroy says matter-of-factly. He squats and wraps his arm around my neck and leans his head on mine. I suck in his cigarette breath. "We'd be fools not to be. I've been through sixteen battles, and I'm still scared every time. But that doesn't mean we won't be brave." He stands, and I breathe in the fresh air. "But I don't want any foolhardiness. I'll just be happy to get back in one piece."

Ellis draws in and makes his cigarette glow again. "Don't you think God's on our side, Conroy?" Ellis's voice drops low and serious. "I mean, I pray every night. I mean, I haven't read all the Good Book, but I know somewhere it says that killing a man is wrong." He flicks his finger against his cigarette, and black ashes rain down. "But, I mean, there's a difference between murder and killing in war, don't you think?"

"I don't know," Conroy says slowly. "Seems like killing is killing, no matter what the motivation. But we're soldiers . . . ."

"I think you're wrong on that, Conroy." Ellis drops his cigarette butt on the ground and grinds it with his boot. "But I'm not going to argue with you about it. But I think God's got to be on our side. I mean, those Germans, they started all this mess."

"What about those Germans, Ellis?" Conroy flips his own ashes onto the ground. "I mean the soldiers in the trenches, not the government in the plush offices back home. There's probably some German fool sitting up there on the ridge saying the same thing to his *kamerad*. I guarantee it."

"But we're *morally* right. God won't let us lose."

"And just like I just said, the Germans probably tell each other the same thing. They think God is on their side."

"Well, one of us is wrong."

"Or else, we're both wrong. I don't see God taking sides in this. I can't imagine him supporting one group slaughtering the other one for any reason."

"Well, I've gotta believe we're right." Frustration rises in his voice. "I need to believe that." Ellis spits on the ground, then turns back and joins the others at the fire.

Conroy slides down and leans back against the trunk. He stubs out his cigarette and pulls me into his lap. He rubs my neck and looks up through the naked branches toward the dark sky. The clouds have parted, and a few stars peek down. We sit silently for a long while as he methodically strokes my back.

Killing -- right? wrong? If you're not hungry or in danger, why do you need to kill?

Sometimes I don't understand humans.

PART FIVE - Partners and Heroes

28

Days and nights pass, and I hear Conroy and the boys talk about more and more men amassing in the area. Even the medics seem to grow in numbers, as well as the stack of stretchers in front of the camp. The boys are jittery like puppies and talk about something big about to happen. Some of the new ones, like Arnie, keep up their bragging, but others look anxious. Some say "big dogs" named General Pershing and Colonel Patton are coming, but I'm still the only four-legged soldier I see.

Tension sifts through the air. As I try to rest underneath Conroy's cot, my paw itches. So, I nip it, in tiny bites, over and over, until it hurts. Then I sleep.

Shuffles and chatter outside the tent wake me a little later. Conroy leaps out of bed and sticks his head out the door. I scramble over beside him. It's still dark outside. He reaches down and scratches my ear. His muscles are tense. His heart beats fast and loud. My blood tingles with excitement.

"Big day, Partner," Conroy tells me. "Big battle coming up." He and the boys shoulder their weapons and head out.

The night is clear; the guns are silent. Occasionally, an enemy flare flies up and spreads a ghostly glare over the scene, as we wait for what seems like hours. Twilight creeps in, and the sky turns a dull slab of gray. At last, the first streaks of dawn show in the sky, and whispered orders send us to our positions along the trench.

My insides are jumpy, and it's hard to be still. I pace around the legs of my boys. The minutes drag slowly, each second seeming an hour, each minute an eternity, as I sense the nervousness and raw fear among the boys. I sniff the crotches of the new boys, so I'll know them on the field. Young Stan reaches down and scratches my ear, and I feel a tremor run through his body. But all is silent as a grave.

The boys' whispered prayers now are not for heroism but for courage – and for survival.

Familiar smells of mud, sweat, and gunpowder drift through my nostrils as I pace. My ears flicker, alert.

Boom!

Shells blast the quiet and lash the ground with fury. Each piece of flying shrapnel searches for an unprotected head. Stan pushes his head tight against the parapet. Loose dirt rolls off his helmet and mats my fur. Resisting the urge to shake, I stand statue-still as all my boys crouch tightly against the walls. A young soldier sits curled in the corner, knees almost to his chin, occasionally cursing or muttering, "The next one'll get us." But he remains motionless. Conroy leans against the trench wall, his eyes mere slits as he watches me and listens.

From the field ahead come cries of pain, and stretcher-bearers push backward and forward to collect and dress the wounded. The sick, sweet, smell of blood grows more pungent with the dirt and smoke.

The bombardment slowly ebbs, and the boys whisper that it's time to move – to join the fray. Quiet as cats, we snake down the trench. One boy trips over a loose helmet that has rolled in from a fallen soldier. Without missing a step, another boy, who has lost his own helmet, grabs it up and puts it on.

An ambulance unit approaches, drawing the enemy's attention, who immediately snipes us with "whizz-bangs."

We hit the ground and seek cover. A shell strikes the sandbags nearby, and a second one bursts in the trench up ahead. One man falls instantly, and the explosion blows Conroy off his feet. I *yelp!* and dart toward him. Then he's gone — in the thick, suffocating cloud of yellow fumes. I hear his cough. I snap my head to the left and see him stand again as the dirt and cloud settle.

I push against his leg, and he gives me a brief stroke before plodding forward, staggering slightly and in a half-daze. The nerve-wracking shelling continues to pound around us as Conroy's step grows steadier.

Still, more stretcher-bearers file back from the front lines, and with each group, I feel a shudder spread through my boys.

"Our turn is coming, Partner," Conroy whispers as he peers over the parapet.

The enemy finally tires, and an eeriness sets in toward the late afternoon.

Our orders come, and we're on the move. We scramble over the top and across the shell-torn hill by the railway. All is silent except the steady and determined crunch of boots of Conroy and my boys. The terrain is difficult to navigate, pitted with old trenches and covered with tangled masses of rusty wire.

My skin buzzes as I scout left and right for the enemy, alert for shells overhead. I hear no wildlife; crows and rats still hide from the morning's barrage of bullets. We skirt the edge of a large crater, flat-bottomed like a frying pan, sadly strewn with bodies of soldiers. The cavity smells of mud and blood and decaying flesh – the smell of death. We trudge on.

At last, we meet the other soldiers and ready our weapons for attack.

Overhead I hear a roar and see a giant silver bird with a big black cross on each underwing. As it flies low overhead, it dips its wing, and I can see the figures of two humans inside.

"Down!" The Captain yells across the field.

Seconds later, with a tremendous *Boom*! the earth erupts in a fountain of dirt and rock. A shiver of fear runs down my back as I crouch next to Conroy. I want to bite my paw, but Conroy wraps his arm tight around my neck.

Soon shells burst from behind us as our own gunners fire back, and we watch the fountains erupt along the enemy lines. We wait – guns ready, bayonets affixed. The pounding continues, and we huddle. At last, there is a lull in the fire.

"Okay, partner. You ready?" Conroy scratches behind my ear. My skin quivers. He pats my chest and adjusts his pack and rifle. He is crouched and ready.

"Charge!" The order echoes down the lines, and my boys and hundreds of fellow soldiers leave their cover and surge toward the enemy lines.

The Germans charge toward us, like a thousand locusts swarming the field, amidst the *rat-a-tat-tat* of machine guns and the *booms* of mortars. Soldiers scream in agony as they fall left and right. Still, we plow forward.

Boom! Dirt and rock burst up from the ground. Stan flies up and lands with a thud. I rush over and nuzzle his neck. He's alive. He groans and grabs his ears with his fists, rolling in the dirt.

"Can't hear!" he yells. "I can't hear!"

"Easy, Stan." Conroy drops beside him. He pats Stan's arm, making motions, then yells at Ellis.

"Ellis! Grab a medic!" The terror on Stan's face relaxes a little when he sees the medic.

"Concussion," says the medic. "Busted his eardrum." He helps him stand and leads him back. Stan hangs onto his ear with his fist.

Conroy scans the field for our boys still charging. His eyes flash.

"Let's go!"

I bound among my boys as shells throw up shrapnel and chunks of smoking earth around us.

The new boys tear out ahead, howling like crazed beasts. They attack anything and everything near them – wildly jabbing, clubbing, slicing, shooting. And always howling. Howling in fear. Howling in anger. Howling, killing, like rabid dogs. I recognize the beast inside them.

Voom! A shell explodes at their feet. Arnie's arms fly up, his rifle drops, and he hits the ground. His face is gone. His partner lies beside him, his arm wrenched from his shoulder, the last of his life's blood pooling around him.

Conroy! Where's Conroy?

Through the haze of battle, I find him, and we charge on. Bullets strike the dirt in front of us as we crisscross the field. I stay close on Conroy's heels. The air snaps around me. Then a bullet kicks a rock into my jaw.

Yelp! I trip, hit the ground, and roll over. I scramble up and start again. Hearing my cry, Conroy pauses for just a second and glances back.

But that second is enough. A rifle cracks. Conroy's head jerks back – and he reels backward to the ground.

I'm at his side instantly, barking, licking his face. He lifts his hand. He rolls his head toward me; then his hand drops -- and his eyes close.

I tug his hand. I lick his face. I can't wake him. I whine. I pull at his arm. I feel another powerful arm scoop me up. I struggle as I hear Ellis's voice. "It's okay, Stubby, it's okay. Let the medics get him." As he speaks, the stretcher-bearers arrive.

Ellis lowers me and helps the medic lift Conroy onto the stretcher; then, the two trot toward the ambulance line. I follow close on their heels. As they load him into the ambulance, I jump in and squeeze to the side. The medic brushes me out and slams the door.

The ambulance rolls down the road. I start to chase.

"Stubby!" I stop at my name. Ellis grabs my collar.

The ambulance grows smaller and smaller and finally disappears in the distance.

"C'mon, boy." Ellis scoops me up and heads back across the field. "He'll be all right." Despite my whimpers and squirms, he holds me tight. His voice is steady, but I can smell his unease. "C'mon, boy. We've got a war to win."

He brightens his voice. "We've got those *Boche* on the run, fella'. Now we're gonna win. We're gonna be heroes."

We stop where Conroy fell, and Ellis lowers me to the ground. I nuzzle Conroy's pack, sucking in his scent. Conroy's helmet lies in the mud. I run over and sniff it and whimper. I push it over and lick it, and taste gunpowder around a small round hole on the side.

Ellis picks up Conroy's rifle. "C'mon, Stubby. Let's go."

My legs won't move. I look up at Ellis. I look down the road where they took Conroy. I look back to Ellis. Back toward Conroy.

Conroy. My partner.

I turn and take off.

Blood races to my heart and my belly. My legs pump hard. I have only one goal.

Conroy.

STUBBY'S WAR

29

I bound down the road, sailing along the field. Ellis calls after me, but I keep running – after the ambulance – after Conroy.

I leap over the muddy pocks in the road and race past the wagons and soldiers. Another ambulance passes me, its tires dropping in a puddle and spattering mud in my face. I shake my head, clear my eyes, and keep running. Toward *Conroy*.

Up and down, up and down, my legs churn as I gallop at full speed. But the rear of the ambulance grows smaller and smaller in the distance.

My lungs burn. My thighs burn. My tongue is parched with thirst. I need water. Beneath my paws, the beaten grass is cold and wet. The shell-scarred road is full of mud holes, but the water is brown and thick. I spot a small pool collected in some tree roots along the roadside.

I lap greedily, slaking my thirst.

From behind, I hear the distant boom of the shelling. This far from the battlefront, the scent of blood is faint. I smell human sweat – and the sweat of horses – but no scent of Conroy. I take off again in the direction of the ambulance.

Abandoned wagons with broken wheels litter the sides of the road, along with discarded harnesses or other gear no longer needed. An occasional ambulance roars to the front, but I skirt to the side and out of the way.

Supply wagons, pulled by tired steeds, plod toward the front. When I spot a mess wagon, my stomach growls, but the soldiers don't know me, so I crouch under a bush until they pass.

Night falls, and I am again alone on the road. My throat burns, and my legs quiver from the run. I choose a big pine a few yards off the road, paw the straw underneath, and lie down to rest.

A full moon slides out from the clouds. The sounds of war are replaced by the scents and sounds of the forest. A twig breaks, and I spot a deer nibbling a green leaf. Holding an acorn in its open mouth, a squirrel circles around the trunk and darts up a nearby oak. Rats scurry among the wet leaves underneath. My nose twitches at their scent. My stomach growls, but exhaustion wins over hunger, and I rest, panting.

Hrff. Hrff. A deep grunt wakes me. In the dark, my ears perk up. I detect the scent of an animal, but not deer, nor horse, nor even rat. My hair stands erect on my neck. Another grunt. I cock my head in the direction of the sound.

Just beyond the shadow of the trees, I spot a large grey-black figure, as tall as a deer but heavier. In the darkness, yellow slits of eyes glare at me. My ears lie back, and my lips pull back to bare my teeth. I narrow my eyes and study the intruder. I sniff a hog-like odor, but this massive hulk is no barn animal. Long, sharp tusks protrude from its jaws as if they could rip through my flesh. I decide I am no match and back away.

The beast snorts and paws the ground. With a sudden piercing cry, it charges.

I flip around and tear out, running toward the road, the beast plowing through the undergrowth behind me. I bound for my life, the snorting getting closer to me. I spot a broken wagon and, with a shot of fear, leap up on the back and clamor to the top.

The beast slams the wagon corner with its shoulder. The impact knocks me off my feet, but the wagon holds. The beast flings its large head from side to side. It circles the wagon. It snuffs around, digging up the ground at the broken wheels. It backs away. It glowers in rage.

My legs and chest quiver at the sight of the beast. At the end of a long, narrow snout, its nostrils glisten. Ragged, pointed ears – caked with blood – stand erect, with coarse bristles sticking up like needles. From its powerful shoulders to its thick hind legs, raised hairs run down the middle of its scarred back. The monster grunts, and slobber drips.

The beast paces and grunts deeply. Whimpering, I turn in circles on the wagon seat, searching for a way out. I shiver and hear the rapid *thump, thump, thump* of my heart.

Crack! A rifle shot pierces the air, followed by a piercing squeal of the monster. It flings its head wildly and takes off running, emitting a loud, huffing *Ukh! Ukh! Ukh!*

Crack! A second shot. The beast lets loose an ear-splitting squeal.

Its front legs crumple – and the beast drops with a

heavy thud.

I look back in the direction of the shot. A boy, smaller than my soldier boys, is silhouetted in the moonlight, lowering a rifle. Another larger form stands beside him and pats the boy's shoulder. I hear his voice: "Good shot, son. That'll feed us for a while."

I glance back at the unmoving monster. I tear out in a run down the road.

On and on, I run through the night, stopping only to lap water from the pools beneath the trees. The night wears on, and my muscles burn and ache. My chest heaves as I suck air. I stay focused on only one thought:

Conroy. Conroy needs me. I need Conroy.

Sometime after midnight, I make it to the medical camp. All is quiet. An ambulance truck is parked by the front door of a large tent, but no one is around. I paw at the tent, but it's shut tight. I sniff around the edges and pick up familiar smells of blood and antiseptic and infection and death – and a shiver of worry makes its way down my spine. With a low whimper, I scratch at the door. No answer. My tail droops. I return to the trees. I make a nest of leaves and wait for dawn.

The morning sky is turning pink when I hear medics returning for their shifts. One soldier pulls open the rear door of the truck. Another soldier ties back the hospital tent opening.

"Let's get these guys loaded," a medic says. "I'd like to make it to Paris by nightfall, and these muddy roads don't make it easy."

I belly-crawl underneath the truck, so I can watch for Conroy.

The medics go into the tent and return with a soldier on a stretcher. I sniff. Not Conroy. They load the soldier in the truck and return to the tent for another. Still not

Conroy. The medics load two more stretchers and guide walking patients to the truck. The last one comes out of the tent, teetering as he walks, half of his head circled in white bandages. A familiar scent floods my nose. *Conroy*!

I scramble out from under the truck with a sharp bark and bound over to Conroy. I jump on his leg. I lick his hand. *Conroy*! I *yip*!

"Get that dog out of here!" A big, barrel-shaped medic kicks me to the side.

A sour rot fills my belly. *I can't lose Conroy.*

With my feet planted and my ears laid back, I growl at the medic.

No! You can't take my Conroy! No! I snap and bark.

The medic picks up a stick and draws back his arm.

"Wait! No! That's Stubby!" Conroy props against a stretcher as he calls out. "He's mine!" His breathing is heavy. His head lolls to one side.

"I don't care whose he is. He's got to get out of the way," the medic growls.

"What's going on out here?" A commanding female voice calls from the tent door. She grabs Conroy and steadies him.

"Just getting rid of a dog, ma'am," the medic answers.

The nurse looks down at me. I recognize her face, her smell. I meet her eyes. Nurse Borg.

"I know this dog," she tells the medic. "That's Stubby. He's a soldier dog, and I hear he's done a lot of good."

"But a dog can't . . ."

"Please . . ." Conroy's voice is weak.

"Let him go," Nurse Borg orders. "Let the officers in Paris decide what to do with him. We'll not abandon him here."

The medic harrumphs. He cuts his eyes at me but puts down the stick. After he helps Conroy into the truck, I jump in and sit at Conroy's feet. The truck engine roars to life. I put my front paws on Conroy's lap. I climb up and lick his face. I nuzzle his ears. He puts his arm around my neck and his face in the thick fur on my chest.

"My partner," Conroy whispers. "My brave partner."

As I peer out the rear window, the people and the camp and the war grow small and smaller until they are a tiny dot and then disappear.

With Conroy, I rumble down the dirt road toward Paris.

PART SIX - The Real Stubby

We leave our story of Stubby as he rides away from the war toward Paris with his partner, Conroy. But that's not the end of Stubby's story. Conroy was wounded on November 2, 1918, just nine days before the Armistice was signed, officially ending the war. But Stubby has many adventures yet to come. Let's look below at what happened to the historical war hero named Stubby.

The real Stubby fought in 17 battles. He fought in the trenches along with his human, J. Robert "Bob" Conroy, and the other "Doughboys" of the 102nd Infantry Battalion, 26th Division. He was gassed and struck with shrapnel. While in the hospital, he comforted the wounded soldiers. Back in the trenches, he used his superior nose and ears to warn of incoming gas shells. He led Conroy and his men through the dangerous "No Man's Land" to find wounded soldiers. He even captured a German spy.

The Great War finally ended, but Stubby's adventures did not. Newspapers across the United States chronicled the life of this heroic dog who captured the imagination and hearts of Americans recovering from the horrific war. The headlines tell the story of Stubby and how he became the most decorated and most famous dog of his time.

A few weeks after Armistice Day, President Woodrow Wilson visited the American Expeditionary Force in Paris, France. This included Stubby's 102nd Regiment. General Pershing opened the event, and the President addressed the troops. This was Christmas Day, 1918. The President met many of the soldiers during the day, shaking hands and greeting representatives of all the regiments. Reportedly, this included "shaking paws" with one particular four-legged hero, Stubby. President Wilson was the first of three Presidents that Stubby would meet in the years after the war.

Sergeant Stubby in his coat bearing his many medals.
Photo source: WikiCommons

As we learned, Stubby was given a special chamois coat made by the women of the village of Chateau Teirrey. On it, they embroidered the flags of the Allies. As the war ended, the medals sewn to the coat began to add up.

General John Pershing awards Stubby a medal. *Photo source: WikiCommons*

Like many other wounded veterans, Stubby's master, Robert Conroy, was awarded a wound stripe, three gold service chevrons (one for every six months of overseas service, and a victory medal. Conroy decided that Stubby needed to be honored, too, and he pinned his medals on Stubby's coat.

Stubby's victory medal included five crossbars clipped over a rainbow ribbon. These represented the five major engagements: Champagne-Marne, Aisne-Marne, St. Mihiel, Meuse-Argonne, and the "Defensive Sector." Overall, Stubby fought in 17 battles. Just like many human soldiers, his right shoulder bore a wound stripe, and the left held the service chevrons.

Additionally, he was given Y.D. (Yankee Division) patches for each of the shoulders of his coat. Other metals were still to come.

Stubby shows off his medals, including the mysterious Iron Cross hanging in the back. His fellow soldiers thought that was best place for the German medal. *Photo source: WikiCommons*

Stubby and Conroy and the 102nd Regiment arrived back in the United States in April 1919. The group was met with hugs and waves from friends, family, and many Americans eager to welcome the heroes home.

Just a couple of weeks later, Stubby led the boys of the 102nd Regiment in a victory parade through the streets of Boston, celebrating the homecoming of the Yankee Division.

On April 25, 1919, the *New York Times* headline announced, "Boston Welcomes Yankee Boys Home." Stubby's unit headed the parade.

The article below describes the fanfare of the day as thousands watched from the grandstands:

26th Division Gets Greatest Demonstration in the History of the City.

> Airplanes soared overhead, cannon thundered their salutes, bands at frequent intervals along the line of march mingled their music with the martial crash of drum and bugle corps, and 1,000,000 throats cheered themselves hoarse. Overhead floated American and allied flags, and from upper windows and roofs, the troops were showered with confetti and streamers . . .
>
> Marching along with the brave soldiers and horses were goats and dogs, "all wearing their service

stripes." One four-legged trench soldier stood out, "wearing five service stripes."

In her book, *Stubby the War Dog,* Ann Bausum describes Stubby leading the parade:

> Stubby walked in a place of honor with the 102nd Regiment, accompanying its color guard display of ceremonial flags. As each contingent of troops reached the reviewing stand, marchers would have responded to the parade command of "eyes right" by turning their heads toward the dignitaries in a sign of respect. Stubby understood this command, so he must have turned his head, too. Then at the appropriate time, he would have faced frontward again and continued walking in formation until commanded to stop.

Conroy received an honorable discharge from the military April 26, 1919, and he and Stubby traveled through several cities to lead victory celebrations.

On May 8, 1919, Stubby became a lifetime member of the Y.M.C.A. His membership card said it was "Good for Three Bones A Day." Conroy's hometown newspaper, *Hartford Courant,* ran the article with the following headline:

102nd Mascot Made Life Member of Y.M.C.A.

The Y.M.C.A initiated a new lifetime member yesterday morning when Stubby, the Boston bull terrier and the official mascot of the 102nd United States Infantry, was given his membership card after being examined and pronounced physically fit . . . He will always be sure of a place to sleep in the Hartford "Y." This evening at the new members' banquet at Jewell Hall "Stubby" will have a special place at the table with his favorite chow."

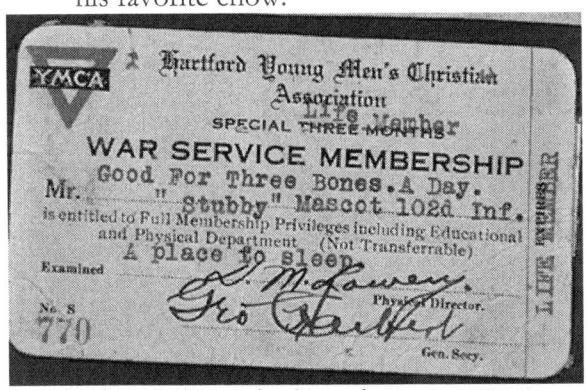

Stubby's YMCA membership card   *Photo source: WikiCommons*

In November 1919, Stubby went with Conroy to the first-ever convention of the American Legion in Minneapolis, Minnesota. This newly-formed organization was formed to serve the veterans of what will become known as World War I. He continued the tradition of marching with the Legionnaires through 1924, when *The Minneapolis Tribune* ran this headline:

'Stubby' Has Hiked with His Pals on Every Parade Route.

Two years later, *The Bridgeport Telegram* (Bridgeport, Connecticut) announced that the American Legion made Stubby a member:

"Stubby," World War Dog, Joins Legion

Even though Stubby was technically a mutt or mixed-breed dog, Conroy entered him in the Eastern Dog Show in Boston the next year and was awarded a special Hero Dog Award. *The Hartford Courant* ran the story:

"Stubby," Y.D. Mascot, Wins More Honors

> "Stubby," the famous mascot of the Yankee Division and now owned by James R. Conroy of this city, had a share in the victory over the Kaiser's army and last week at the Boston dog show took a blue ribbon in his class. Stubby has received more attention, probably in the United States. He has been looked upon by more people than any other dog that went through the war."

In the fall of 1920, Stubby's adventures began a new chapter. Conroy began studying at Catholic University, and Stubby became the school football mascot. *The Washington Post* described how Stubby has his own way of playing the game:

"Stubby, War Dog Hero, will be C.U. Mascot in State Game

As far as a mascot is concerned, the success of the Catholic University football team in their annual clash with Maryland State is assured. Stubby, the wonder dog of the A.E.F. in France, is quartered at the Brookland Institute, taking a well-deserved rest after three years of active service on the battlefields of France.... Stubby's delight is in chasing a football. There is no such word as down when he is chasing the pigskin. He will be at the game next Saturday rooting hard for Harry Robb's light but aggressive gridironers."

When Conroy entered law school that same year at Georgetown University in Washington, D.C., Stubby became the mascot of their football team and served with their team for several years:

A.E.F. Bull Pup Latest Mascot at Georgetown

Laddie Boy's rival is in town to stay. "Stubby," the fighting bull pup of the A.E.F., who sports three gold chevrons and a wound stripe, is going on active duty this year as the official mascot for Georgetown University.... He's happy in his new job as a mascot for Georgetown and intends to follow the pigskin at every contest during the season.

In March 1921, Stubby received another special award from the Boston Terrier Club. However, in the news article, his name is spelled as "Stuffy," and his reputation has grown to say that in the war, he was wounded five times, or "stopped five bullets"! Notice how his legend has grown:

"Stuffy," Real War Dog, Is Booked for Exhibition Here

....That all was not beer and skittles, however, is shown by the fact that "Stuffy" was wounded five times in action. He accompanied his Doughboy friends wherever they went, even if that meant attacking the enemy. That is how he happened to stop five bullets. But he was "toughy" as well as "Stuffy," and he recovered each time to proudly return from the war.

A couple of months later, Stubby leads his group in a parade for wounded veterans on the grounds of the White House. Here he meets his second President, Warren G. Harding. This is described in *Boston Post's* story:

Yankee Division Veterans Parade with the "Old Guy"

....Lieutenant-Colonel William Sullivan marched at the head of the 102nd Infantry, composed largely of Connecticut troops, and he shared applause with "Stubby," famed dog mascot of the Regiment, wearing two wound stripes and medals variously accumulated by members of the Regiment. Attached to the blanket which bore his decorations was a small American flag, and the dog marched in perfect alignment and with his head held erect as though he realized his responsibility. Many spectators uncovered their heads for the tiny flag with as much respect as when the bigger banners passed.

Stubby riding on float in parade *(Photo in public domain)*

Stubby and Conroy became active with the American Humane Society. In one of the more famous photographs of Stubby, he is pictured riding a special float in a Humane Society parade. Again, he had on his blanket with a tiny flag mounted on its back. The President and Mrs. Harding and their dog, Laddie Boy, also rode in the parade.

Another medal is attached to Stubby's blanket the next month, when Stubby is honored by General John J. Pershing on behalf of the American Humane Society, an animal rights group.

According to The *New York Times* article, General Pershing made an impromptu speech praising Stubby's valor in war. Stubby's reaction? "…Stubby made no reply. He merely licked his chops and wagged his diminutive tail."

In 1922, Stubby and Conroy attended American Legion conventions in Kansas City, Minneapolis, Omaha, and New Orleans. See if you can spot the errors recorded about Stubby in this *Washington Times* article about the New Orleans convention:

Legion Party "Wallowing" Through Dixie

"Stubby," a thorough-bred Boston bull terrier, official mascot of the one hundred ninety-second infantry of the forty-second "Yankee" division, in charge of Sergt. Bob Conroy, is receiving no end of attention of both passengers and crew. Stubby was in no less than five combats with his A.E.F. maneuvers, and emerged with a single scar, a slight flesh wound in his right front leg. This canine has been decorated by all the allied countries....

Before the end of the year, Stubby's famous blanket opened doors previously shut to canine guests. The New York Times describes his welcome into the Hotel Majestic:

Hero Dog Hotel Guest: Majestic Lifts Ban for "Stubby: Decorated by Pershing

For the first time since Copeland Townsend acquired the Hotel Majestic, the hard and fast rule prohibiting dogs in the hotel was waived yesterday for "Stubby: the

> famous mascot of New England's veteran Twenty-Sixth (Yankee) Division, who arrived there en route to Washington. ... When "Stubby's" blanket, laden with medals and decorations, some of which were placed there by General Pershing, General Clarence Edwards, and President Harding, was exhibited, he was not only admitted to the hotel, but was given the best accommodations available and had a special chef assigned to attend to his gustatory desires.

In 1924, Stubby met his third President when he was invited to the White House to meet President Calvin Coolidge.

In 1925, the aging Stubby attended his final American Legion convention in Omaha, Nebraska. He will, however, forever be a part of their history, and his story is still preserved at their headquarters.

In 1926, cradled in his partner's arms, Stubby died at home. His obituaries echoed across the nation in newspapers great and small.

STUBBY'S WAR

Stubby's brick at Liberty Memorial in Kansas City

Perhaps Stubby's most famous obituary is the one reprinted below, published in *The New York Times*, March 16, 1926.

STUBBY OF A.E.F. ENTERS VALHALLA

Tramp Dog of No Pedigree Took Part In the Big Parade in France

Stubby is dead. He was only a dog and unpedigreed at that, but he was the most famous mascot in the A.E.F. Stubby took part in four major offensives, was wounded and gassed.

He captured a German Spy and won more medals than any other soldier dog. He led the American Legion parades and was known to three Presidents. He was, indisputably, a fighting dog. His Arlington is to be the Smithsonian Institution.

Early in life Stubby longed for a career. Realizing the value of education, the brindle and white "bull terrier" abandoned his nomadic life for that of a student. Selecting Yale University as his alma mater, he was soon recognized there as a prodigy. His progress, however, was interrupted.

America entered the war and the First Connecticut Regiment, later merged into the 102d Infantry, Twenty-sixth Division, was ordered to Yale field for training.

Though delighted with his intellectual environment and his frolics in the huge Bowl, Stubby came to the conclusion that he ought to do his bit by his country. It was hard, after five peregrinating years, during which he had often been hungry and cold, to leave the only of peace and hospitality he had ever found. But in such a time, when men were parting from mothers and wives to defend the honor of Uncle

(See Obituary, pt. 2)

Obituary, part 2:

Sam, was he, a mere wanderer without dependents, to think of self?

Stubby joined up. One morning a bugle sounded the departure from camp. Crammed into a train loaded with equipment, he was started South. He knew not where he was speeding.

His recent contacts with scholasticism, however, stood him in good stead. Tennyson had said something memorable--"His not to reason why, his but to do and die."

At Newport News, the soldiers were hustled aboard a transport. Here difficulties arose. Stubby was not on the roster. He had no enlistment card. The officers were stern and unknown to him. Corporal J. Robert Conroy perceived his hangdog look and was touched. Wrapping him into the greatcoat slung on his arm and admonishing him to be quiet, he smuggled him up the gangway.

Stubby lay still, with bated breath, until released into a coal bunker. Without diminishing allegiance to all his comrades, Stubby, from that moment adopted Conroy as his master.

On February 5, 1918, he entered the front lines of the Chemin des Dames sector, north of Soissons, where he was under fire night and day for more than a month. The noise and strain that shattered the nerves of many of his comrades did not impair Stubby's spirits. Not because he was unconscious of danger. His angry howl while a battle raged, and his mad canter from one part of the lines to another indicated realization. But he seemed to know that the greatest service he could render was comfort and cheerfulness.

When he deserted the front lines, it was to keep a wounded soldier company in the corner of a dugout or in the deserted section of a trench. If the suffering doughboy fell asleep, Stubby stayed awake to watch.

In the Chemin des Dames, Stubby captured a German spy and saved a doughboy from a gas attack. Hearing a sound in the stillness of the night, the dog, who guarded sleeplessly, stole out of the trenches and recognized--a German. Attempts by the German to deceive the dog were futile. Seizing his prisoner by the breeches, Stubby held on until help arrived.

Stubby, on other leaves, visited Nice, Monte Carlo, and Nancy.

At Neufchateau, the home of Jeanne d' Arc, he was presented with the first of the many medals he later won in dog shows and Victory loan drives.

Upon his return to the front, he found himself in the thick of the Meuse-Argonne fray, which was to end the war.

Obituary, part. 3:

After Armistice, Stubby spent his time congratulating and being congratulated. Traversing the streets of Paris, he was recognized by hundreds of French, English, Australian and American soldiers. And then, on Christmas Day, at Mandres-en-Basigny, he met President Wilson. Stubby, the dog to whom rank insignia made no difference, offered his paw. Little had he expected that he was to be known and greeted by three Presidents.

Back in his native land, he was demobilized at Camp Devens, Mass., on April 20, 1919. Parading with his famous division in Boston, he was reviewed by Governor Calvin Coolidge.

An acquaintance was started, which was renewed at the American Legion convention at Kansas City in 1921, attended by Vice President Coolidge, and at the convention in Omaha in 1926, attended by President Coolidge.

On parade, Stubby always wore the embroidered chamois blanket presented to him by admiring Frenchwomen and decorated with service chevrons, medals, pins, buttons, and a galaxy of souvenirs. On the end of his modernly bobbed tail, a German iron cross was appended, the possession of which Stubby never explained.

Conroy's decision to study law at Georgetown University brought him and Stubby to Washington.

There Conroy became secretary to Representative E. Hart Fenn of Connecticut, and Stubby met Representative William P. Connery Jr. of Massachusetts and B. Carroll Reece of Tennessee, old friends from the Twenty-sixth Division, in Congress. His buddies were coming into prominence.

One day Stubby encountered Major M.D. Arnold and Captain J.W. Boyer, both of the old Y. D. Besides being painted by Charles Ayer Whipple, artist of the Capitol, Stubby had the distinction of being photographed with General Pershing.

STUBBY'S WAR

STUBBY'S WAR

PART SEVEN - The War in Pictures

As the first major war of the 20th century, World War One was covered closely in newspapers in America and around the world.

(All photos in public domain)

The spark that ignited World War I happened on June 28, 1914, when a young Serbian shot and killed

Archduke Franz Ferdinand, the heir to the Austrian-Hungarian Empire. Within a month, Austria invaded Serbia. Alliances formed among the countries of Europe, and soon the world was involved. The assassination made *New York Times* headlines.

America wanted to stay out of the war. The sinking of the *Lusitania* played a major role in influencing America to enter the war, but they didn't join the war for two more years. The trigger that brought them in was when Germany sunk ten American merchant ships. America declared war April 6, 1917.

The "Stamp out the Kaiser" poster was one of the most famous propaganda posters Stubby would have seen. World War One was the first war in which propaganda played a major role, both in influencing young men to join the military and in generating support for the war among those left at home.

Thousands of young men joined the armies across Europe and the United States, all eager to "stamp out the Kaiser." However, they quickly learned that military life was tough – living quarters were rough and the fighting was horrific. Thousands of the young men did not survive.

At right, British camp at Battle of Somme, France, 1916.

Short-legged Stubby and even long-legged human soldiers had difficulty marching in the mud. The picture above shows some French soldiers trying to get their truck loose from the mud.

A War of "Firsts"

World War One has been called the Great War and the War to End All Wars. It certainly changed the history of the civilized world. It also saw the first arrival of many weapons and practices.

1. First truly "global warfare" involving more than 30 countries across four different continents.
2. First major use of chemical weapons (gas and flamethrowers)
3. Widespread use of weapons of mass destruction – artillery, machine guns, tanks, aerial bombing
4. Widespread Trench warfare
5. Major use of propaganda for recruitment and support at home and later for anti-war sentiments
6. Massive social upheaval as women went to work to replace men who had gone to war.

Weapons of War

British artillery in action

George S. Patton in front of tank– France, Signal Core

World War One saw the first use of some weapons of mass destruction. Grenades, artillery, machine guns, tanks, and aerial bombing (in addition to traditional combat and disease and exposure) took the lives of over 16 million soldiers across four continents.

Although toxic chemicals had been used for many years before World War One, this was the first time they were used on a large scale for many fatalities. The primary chemical weapon was a toxic mustard gas that floated over the trenches and killed, injured, or demoralized the soldiers. After being gassed for the first time, Stubby learned to detect the coming gas and warn his fellow soldiers in time for them to put on their gas masks.

British 55th Division soldiers blinded by poison gas. This scene is described by Stubby in the section "Wounded Warriors."

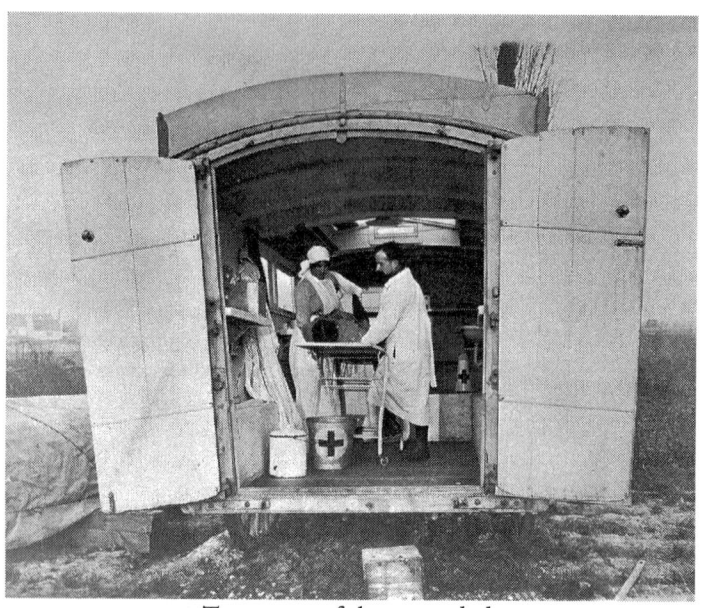

Transport of the wounded.

Bristol Scout plane (above). On 25 July 1915 Captain Lanoe Hawker attacked three German aircraft. His first attack sent a German aircraft spinning down. His second drove an aircraft to the ground badly damaged, and the third, an Albatros C, burst into flames and crashed. For this feat Capt. Hawker was awarded the Victoria Cross.

SS (sea scout) class blimp was first introduced in 1915.

Trench Warfare

The trench system developed in World War One when the Germans' initial offensive was stopped in 1914. Both armies dug in, using trenches, and trying to outflank each other. Historians estimate that over 500 miles of interconnected trenches were dug for cover and transport.

Once the trenches were complete, there was nothing left to do but slug it out. Artillery, aerial bombing, and chemical weapons were used to break the stalemate that the trenches caused. Tanks were specifically developed to crush through the trenches.

(Note: World War One was not the first use of trenches. The Seize of Petersburg in American Civil War saw over nine months of warfare in over 30 miles of trenches.)

British soldiers use a crude periscope to look above the edge of the trench (above).

American soldiers rest in a crude trench (above).

A soldier keeps watch over the parapet (above).

Soldiers tramp through flooded communications trench (above). Soldiers crawl toward the front (below).

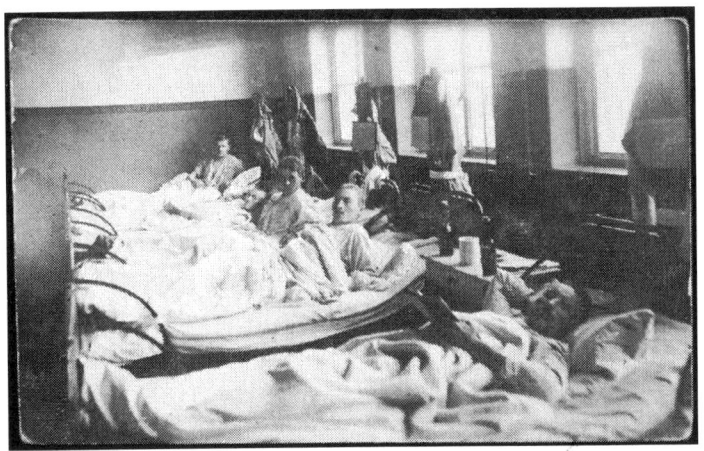

Soldiers recover in a hospital (above).

In the last scene of our story, Stubby jumps aboard an ambulance and heads toward Paris. In the picture above, an American ambulance heads toward Verdon. A shell explodes in the distance.

(Photos source: Library of Congress, public domain.)

Peace at Last

On the 11th hour of the 11th day of the 11th month, Armistice was signed, and the Great War ended. The war had claimed millions of lives and toppled four empires. Our boys, and Stubby, were eager to come home.

Stubby and Conroy march in a victory parade.

RESOURCES FOR FURTHER STUDY

A journalist once said that "Stubby's story is the story of all our brave soldiers in The Great War." In this 'war to end all wars,' we saw thousands of our soldiers die as we used weapons of mass destruction for the first time with the introduction of machine guns, tanks, and airplanes. We also used chemical weapons for the first time.

In this sea of statistics, it's often easy to lose sight of the solitary soldier who succumbed to the patriotic propaganda and volunteered his service only to realize the real hell of war as thousands of our boys rolled 'over the top' into the waiting eyes of machine guns and tanks. How does one retain hope and courage in these situations?

Stubby gives us a view from inside the muddy trenches of the war and introduces us to some of the soldiers who fought in the war. He tells of their bravery and the strong friendships formed there.

Stubby was a real dog. His preserved body is now on display in the Smithsonian Museum, along with his coat of many medals and the scrapbook kept by his owner and partner, John Robert 'Bob' Conroy. Many newspaper articles have been written about him. Recently, two nonfiction books about Stubby have been published by National Geographic. Stubby may be a canine, but in many ways, he represents all our Doughboys and their heroism in the war.

In writing this story, I explored a multitude of letters, diaries, journals, and memoirs of our boys in World War One, especially those in the 26th Infantry 'Yankee' Division of 102nd Company. These diaries and journals offered extra adventures that Stubby may not have been a part of, but that did happen to those around him. These references are listed below along with the chapter where the story is included so that you can read the original story and compare Stubby's version. As for a couple of other instances you read, well, let's just say that Stubby sometimes likes to embellish his story a little.

To discover more facts about the real Stubby and our soldiers during the war, check out the nonfiction stories in "For Further Reading" at the end of this book. There, you will also find stories of other brave animal heroes who served with American soldiers during times of war.

CHAPTER REFERENCES

Chapter 6. Dog tags. from Bausum, Ann. *Sergeant Stubby: How a Stray Dog and His Best Friend Helped Win World War I*. New York: National Geographic. 2015.
Missanabee. From Merrill, Charles. *Lucky Charlie: Memoirs of Charles Leo Boucher (Edited)*. Web.

Chapter 8. Stand-to. From Duffy, Michael. "Life in the Trenches." *First World War*. Web.
Apples. From Merrill, Charles. *Lucky Charlie: Memoirs of Charles Leo Boucher (Edited)*. Web.

Chapter 10. False teeth. From Duffy, Michael. "Trenches at Vimy Ridge." *First World War*. 2009. Web. First published *in Everyman at War (1930), edited by C. B. Purdom.*

Chapter 12. Gas. From "The Price of Freedom: Stubby." *National Museum of American History*. Smithsonian Institution. Web.

Chapter 19. Hospital. From La Motte, Ellen N. "This Is How It Was: An American Nurse in France during World

War I." *The Backwash of War*. New York: Putnam, 1934. 19-31. *History Matters*. Web.

Sergeant Curtin poem from Bausum, Ann. *Sergeant Stubby: How a Stray Dog and His Best Friend Helped Win World War I*. New York: National Geographic. 2015. *Spy*. "Stubby the Military Dog." *Connecticut Military Department*. State of Connecticut. Web.

Chapter 21. The Spy. From *Sergeant Curtin's poem* from Bausum, Ann. *Sergeant Stubby: How a Stray Dog and His Best Friend Helped Win World War I*. New York: National Geographic. 2015.

Chapter 22. Forest of Horror. Newton, Willie. "Diary of a Doughboy." *North Carolina Digital History*. Web. First published as "Diary of Willard Newton, July 24–28, 1918." Published in the *Charlotte Observer*, September 19, 1920.

Chapter 23. Tanks. From Duffy, Michael. "When Tanks Fought Tanks." *First World War*. Web.

The Real Stubby.

"102d Mascot Made Life Member of Y.M.C.A." *The Hartford Courant*. (Hartford) 9 May 1919. Web.

"A.E.F. Bull Pup Latest Mascot at Georgetown." *The Washington Times*. 30 September 1921. Web.

Bausum, Ann. *Sergeant Stubby: How a Stray Dog and His Best Friend Helped Win World War I*. New York: National Geographic. 2015.

"Boston Welcomes Yankee Boys Home." *New York Times*. 26 April 1919. Web.

"Dog and Girl Mistress." *The Washington Herald*. 14 May 1921. Web.

"Hero Dog Hotel Guest." *New York Times*. 31 December 1922. Web.

Kane, Gillian. "Meet Sergeant Stubby, America's Original Dog of War." *Slate Magazine*, Slate, 8 May 2014. Web.

"Legion Party 'Wallowing' thru Dixie." *The Washington Times.* 14 October 1922. Web.

"Many Thousand Y.D. Vets Here for Celebration." *Boston Post.* (Boston, Massachusetts) 3 July 1921. Web.

"Medal for Mascot of 26th." *Boston Post.* (Boston, Massachusetts) 7 July 1921. Web.

"Pershing Honors Dog Mascot of A.E.F." *New York Times.* 7 July 1921.

"Stubby, 102d Mascot, Gets Third War Medal Decoration." *The Hartford Courant.* (Hartford, Connecticut) 8 July 1921. Web.

"Stubby of A.E.F. Enters Valhalla." Obituary. *New York Times* 4 April 1926.

"Stubby, Dog Hero, in Parade Today." *The Washington Post.* 11 May 1921. Web.

"Stubby Has Hiked with His Pals on Every Legion Parade Route." *Star Tribune* (Minneapolis, Minnesota) 17 September 1924.

"'Stubby,' Hero Pup Decorated by Pershing." *New York Times.* 17 July 1921.

"Stubby, War Dog Hero, will be C.U. Mascot in State Game." *The Washington Post.* 1 November 1920.

"Stubby, World War Dog, Joins Legion." *The Bridgeport Telegram* (Bridgeport, Connecticut). 12 March 1926. Web.

"Stubby, Y.D. Mascot, Wins More Honors." *The Hartford Courant.* (Hartford, Connecticut) 25 February 1920. Web.

"Yankee Division Veterans' Parade with the 'Old Man' Leading Line." Boston Post. (Boston, Massachusetts) 5 July 1921. Web.

FOR FURTHER READING

Historical Stubby

Bausum, Ann. *Sergeant Stubby: How a Stray Dog and His Best Friend Helped Win World War I and Stole the Heart of a Nation.* New York: National Geographic, 2014.

Bausum, Ann. *Stubby the War Dog: The True Story of World War I's Bravest Dog.* New York: National Geographic, 2014.

George, Isabel. *The Most Decorated Dog in History: Sergeant Stubby.* New York: HarperCollins, 2010.

"The Price of Freedom: Stubby." *Armed Forces History.* National Museum of American History. Smithsonian Institution.

"Stubby of A.E.F. Enters Valhalla." Obituary. *New York Times* 4 April 1926. Web.

World War I – Diaries and Memoirs

Avery, Samuel E. *Soldier's Mail: Letters Home from a Yankee Doughboy 1916-1919.* Web.

Borlin, Jon & David Borlin. *Marion Borlin's Letters from World War One.* Borlin Family. Web.

Burbage. A.M. "Memoirs & Diaries – War Is War – Fear, Friends, and Black Humour." First published in *Everyman at War* (1930), ed. C.B. Purdom. First World War.com. Michael Duffy. Web.

La Motte, Ellen N. "This Is How It Was: An American Nurse in France during World War I." *The Backwash of War.* New York: Putnam, 1934. 19-31. *History Matters.* Web.

Landers, Rich. *Soldier's Mail: Letters Home from a Yankee Doughboy 1916-1919.* Web.

"Marion Borlin Letters from World War I."

Merrill, Charles. *Lucky Charlie: Memoirs of Charles Leo Boucher (Edited).* Web.

Mitchell, F. "Memoirs & Diaries – When Tank Fought Tank." First published in *Everyman at War* (1930), ed. C.B. Purdom. First World War.com. Michael Duffy. Web.

Patterson. James. *World War I: A Day in the Trenches of World War I*. Web

Saunders, Harold. "Memoirs & Diaries – Trenches at Vimy Ridge." First published in *Everyman at War* (1930), ed. C.B. Purdom. First World War.com. Michael Duffy. Web.

War Nurse's Diary, A.: Sketches from a Belgian Field Hospital. 1918. Ebook by Pickle Partners Publishing: 2013.

York, Alvin. *The Diary of Alvin York*.: Alvin York Institute. Web.

World War I – Fiction

Eldridge, Jim. *Flying Ace: Jack Fairfax, Royal Flying Corps, 1915-1918*. New York: Scholastic, 2003.

Hart, Alison. Darling: *Mercy Dog of World War I*. Atlanta: Peachtree, 2013.

Hemingway, Ernest. *A Farewell to Arms*. New York: Charles Scribner's Sons, 1957.

Morpurgo, Michael. *Private Peaceful*. New York: Scholastic Press, 2003.

Remarque, Erich Maria. *All Quiet on the Western Front*. New York: Little, Brown, and Company, 1929.

Wilding, Valerie. *Road to War: A First World War Girl's Diary, 1916*. New York: Scholastic, 2008.

Other Historical Animal Heroes

Morpurgo, Michael. *War Horse*. New York: Scholastic, Inc. 1982.

Smith, Roland. *The Captain's Dog: My Journey with the Lewis and Clarke Tribe*. New York: Houghton Mifflin Harcourt Publishing, 1999.

Note: All photos used in this book are in public domain.

NOTE FROM THE AUTHOR

My one regret in writing this book is that I did not discover Stubby while my grandfather, Robert Stanley Rawding, was still living. I knew he had served in World War One, and I knew that he had enlisted when he was living in Massachusetts.

While looking through the records left after his death, I discovered that he had served in the 26th Yankee Division.

That means that my grandfather probably knew Stubby! Wow! I wish he were here now so that I could ask him if he did. Maybe he somehow sent me the little nudge to explore this amazing story.

While serving with the 26th Division in France during World War One, my grandfather wrote a poem. I honor him and all the American soldiers who fought in the war by reprinting his poem on the following page.

STUBBY'S WAR

At the Marne

Darkness comes stealing over the battlefields of France,
And the hated Hun is driven back with rifle, sword, and dance;
It has taken men and money to defeat these hellish fiends.
Sacrifice shall be our motto till we look on fairer scenes.

Our boys are from New England, the fairest of them all.
They were the first to answer when duty made its call.
And on the eve of battle, all hearts were stout and strong,
Ready for the conflict, which they knew would right a wrong.

The tyrant is defeated, their troops scattered afar;
Old Glory waves majestically as she did in years gone by.
As our boys go marching homeward full of victory, love and pride,
You will notice there a sadness for their comrades which have died.

Time cannot soon erase, or will grieving bring back again
That loved one to the mother, her boy, her love and pride.
He was one who gave his all so that others would be spared.
God bless him and those others, for through them the day was saved.

Robert Stanley Rawding, 1895-1980

ABOUT THE AUTHOR

I have loved stories since the first time I learned to read my Dick and Jane books. Although I grew up poor, I had plenty of books. Each month, I ran down the road to meet the Bookmobile, a big van crammed with books to be checked out by the kids and grownups living on the dusty roads of rural Alabama. The stories in those books took me to faraway lands and daring adventures and opened a world to be explored.

My love of stories continued, and I became a teacher. After many years of teaching others to write their stories, I decided it was time to write my own.

I hope you enjoyed this story of a brave dog who fought with our brave young men during a devastating war. To learn more about these soldiers and this war, visit www.dianeweberbooks.com. I would love to hear your thoughts and ideas about Stubby and about the war. Be sure to message me on the website, and I will message back!

Last – but not least – I would love to hear what you thought about Stubby and my book. A **review** where you found this book would mean the world to me – **writers love reviews –** like Stubby loves bacon! So, love it (or not), **your honest review** would make my day. **Thank you!**

Made in the USA
Columbia, SC
27 September 2024